OVER THE DISTANT MOUNTAIN RANGES

DENNIS W.C. WONG

Over the Distant Mountain Ranges
Copyright © 2024 by Dennis W.C. Wong

ISBN: 979-8990639089 (hc)

ISBN: 979-8990639041 (sc)

ISBN: 979-8990639058 (e)

The views expressed in this book are solely those of the author and do not necessarily reflect the views of the publisher, and the publisher hereby disclaims any responsibility for them.

Life is just a part of living; it will encroach upon your path. Always be ready and prepared for the challenges that may lie ahead. When you approach a fork in the road and cannot decide which way to proceed, digress, and make a U-turn. Take a moment to think about the purpose of your journey, make a decision, and then turn around. Follow your instincts and be confident in yourself. Never regret the choice that you made.

—Dennis W.C. Wong

**Dedicated in Loving Memory
to my sister Debbie
October 18, 1954 - May 06, 2005.**

"Adorned Beauty,"
Adorned beauty,
natural as can be,
precious for all to see,
in spirit, you are free.
Remembering yesterday,
reminiscing this May.
Remembering the years,
the unknown and the fears.
Remembering all that you meant,
and the brief times that we spent.
Remembering our birthday exchanges,
over the distant mountain ranges.
Reflecting on your new outlook,
and the path that you took.
A new beginning unravels;
go placidly in your travels.
Losing you is sad,
but now you're with Dad.

Contents

Dennis W.C. Wong was born at Kapiolani Hospital in Honolulu, Oahu, in the territory of Hawaii in 1951. He found out from a lady in a gift shop that the hospital had to move its Labor and Delivery Department into the basement after the attack on Pearl Harbor, then moved again to the third floor. This was to ensure the safety of the pregnant mothers and their babies, of which he and his mother Katherine were part of.

∞ ∞ ∞

Chapter 1

Life is one of the most beautiful things

Life is one of the most beautiful things when spent with someone who truly loves you. The beauty of life is steeped in its challenges and uncertainties; otherwise, it would be drab, bland, and colorless. And when these challenges and uncertainties face, those one loves and those who love one, life becomes filled with eternal memories, memories that will never end.

She was her parent's favorite and their only child. They didn't have all the good and pleasant things of life. There was one thing they had that even money couldn't buy, and that was true love.

She got down from the foam mattress that she usually slept on and walked out of the house, going straight to the river to wash her face. Her family had that advantage because they lived close to the river. She had always wanted to ask why her parents chose somewhere close to the river, but whenever she tried to ask, she would swallow her question, hoping that one day they would tell her. She was named Lucinda, the daughter of a poor farmer.

"Lucinda, how many times have I warned you not to go close to the river. You can't swim yet; you might drown," Annalise said, shouting at Lucinda as she was already in the river.

1

"I don't know how to swim because you won't allow me. I'm already ten years old, and I want to learn how to swim. The water is so calm, and I feel I have this powerful connection with it," Lucinda replied as she emerged from the water.

"You're only ten and already talking about having a strong connection with the river. Will you get back home before I get mad at you!" Annalise shouted as she watched her daughter stroll back to their building, a stone's throw from the river bank.

Annalise then strolled into the river as she took out the clothes to wash. While doing the laundry, she turned and saw Lucinda standing at the bank looking at her.

"I thought I asked you to go home? What did you come back to do?" Annalise yelled.

"Mom, you're always upset about everything, and besides, it was Dad who asked me to come and keep you company. So, can I step into the river?" Lucinda pleaded.

"No, you can't. Just stay there, and besides, I didn't tell your dad I needed help with the laundry. So please go back home," Annalise said while she turned to continue with her laundry.

"I'm not going back home," Lucinda shrugged and sat down at the riverbank, a little distance from her mom.

"Why is that so, young lady?" Annalise asked.

"It is so because you brought me up never to disobey my father. You always say I should help even without being asked to, but since you wouldn't want me to step into the river, I will wait here and help you carry the clothes home," Lucinda replied, rather adamantly.

Annalise smiled and continued with her laundry silently. Immediately, she finished up, and Lucinda helped her with the clothes as they walked home together. Annalise walked inside and left Lucinda to spread the clothes on the rope so they would dry. When Lucinda finished, she stepped inside and went straight to the kitchen to join her mom.

"Are you through with spreading the clothes?" Annalise asked as she saw Lucinda walk into the kitchen.

"I'm through, Mom," Lucinda replied.

Lucinda walked back into her room, and after what seemed like forever, her mom called her so she could come and eat. Promptly, she joined her parents at the table as they ate quietly.

One thing was sure; love lived here. Lucinda's parents had everything good, nothing valuable to boast of, not even their land. They couldn't afford to get a place to build in the village, and that was why they had chosen somewhere close to the river. Phil and Annalise didn't care about how the world felt about them; they only cared about themselves. Lucinda was their only child, and they treasured her.

When they had finished eating, Lucinda took the plates to the kitchen to wash while her mom and dad went outside to receive some cool breeze on the balcony. When she finished, she went into her room to stay. She had no one to play with, nor any toys or pets. It was her alone and her parents.

It was already late at night as Lucinda's parents walked into her room to kiss her goodnight; when they found out, she was still awake.

"Lucinda, why are you still up? Is there any problem?" Phil asked.

"Can you tell me a story before I go to sleep?" Lucinda requested.

"Sure, that can never be a problem," Annalise said as she sat close to her daughter while Lucinda placed her head on her mother's lap.

"Here we go: Once upon a time, in a faraway kingdom, there lived a young boy who tended to the sheep. He had close to two hundred of them. However, the villagers feared the hyenas. They knew that this animal would always come for their livestock. So anytime the hyenas attacked the village, the villagers would come out in great numbers to chase them back into the forest. On a certain day, this young lad was sitting on the tree feeling bored but thinking nothing in particular. Suddenly, he thought of a prank as he observed his sheep feeding happily on the field of grass before him. Suddenly, he shouted at the top of his voice and called the villagers to come to his rescue. And that the hyenas were about to devour his sheep. The villagers heard his voice and came out in great numbers with several weapons, but were disappointed to see that the young lad had raised a false alarm. Disappointed, they all went home angry as the young lad laughed so hard, feeling proud of the prank he just pulled. Well, he repeated it the next day, and the villagers rushed out again to see it was still mischief, but on the third day, the hyenas attacked his sheep, and when he called on the villagers to help, no one came out. They all thought it was a false alarm. The young lad lost about a hundred of his sheep that night. The ones left were brutally wounded as he walked home with them. He went home and cried himself to stupor. It was an expensive prank that cost him dearly. Here ends my story. So, tell me what you have learned," Annalise said, smiling at Lucinda.

"The first lesson is never to raise a false alarm to kill boredom, and then, one should always be sincere and honest in everything he or she is doing," Lucinda replied.

"That's true. So, my dear, raise no false alarm, and always be true to your words so that whenever you need help, people will come right away to help you. Is that understood?" Annalise asked.

"Yes, Mom," Lucinda said, smiling while Phil was sitting by the side, listening and watching his daughter.

Annalise and Phil eventually kissed her goodnight when they were sure she was fast asleep, and they both walked out of the room into their room, lying on the bed immediately to drift off to sleep. It was their usual daily routine.

On the next morning, Lucinda woke up as usual, and as she stood up from her foam, her back started aching again, which had been ongoing for several days now. Had her parents had the money, they would have gotten her a good bed, as this foam was already flat.

She walked out of the room and made it straight for the river, something that had become her morning ritual, something she hadn't missed for five years now. As early as five years old, Lucinda had gone to the river, and her parents would hurriedly come to bring her home for fear of drowning, but for those five years she was doing, they had never given up on that. She wanted to explore and know what it was like to be inside the water. After the first day, she tried it; she hadn't stopped, although she has never dared to venture into the deeper part of the water.

She washed her face that morning with the river's flowing waters, Lucinda sat on the river bank throwing pebbles into the river, enjoying the spluttering sounds of the pebble's impact on the surface of the river with the ripples they formed.

Annalise and Phil were at the back of the house planting seeds when they heard Lucinda's echoing from the river. They quickly dropped what they were holding as they ran towards the riverside. Lucinda was there, struggling to breathe as she kept shouting her parent's name. Phil jumped into the river and swam to save his daughter from drowning. Phil could grab hold of his daughter and swam back to the river bank. Annalise was in tears, praying that nothing would happen to her daughter. Phil laid Lucinda on the floor as he pressed her stomach, and water was gushing out from her mouth.

"She is alive!" Annalise shouted, as Phil carried Lucinda and went back home. Annalise change her daughter's wet clothes to dry ones. Phil came back and presented a cup of tea to Annalise as he raised Lucinda to drink the hot tea.

"What happened? Have I not warned you countless times never to go close to the river? What were you doing at the deeper part of the river?" Annalise asked, crying.

"You shouldn't be asking her that now. She needs to rest. Just wait until later on. Then you can start asking questions," Phil said.

Annalise managed to put Lucinda to sleep as she and her husband walked out of Lucinda's room and continued to their room. Annalise was still in tears. She couldn't imagine that she was about to lose her daughter. What would have happened if her husband wasn't around?

"Annalise, stop crying. Nothing is wrong with her. She just needs to rest, and she will be okay," Phil assured.

"What would have happened if you were not around or if we didn't get there on time? I would have been holding my daughter's corpse, of course. I have warned her countless times to stop going to the river, but she won't listen to me," Annalise whined.

"She is a little child and is bound to explore her curiosities. She has been going there ever since she was five, so telling her to stop now is a waste of time; rather, we can just caution her never to go to the deeper part of the river. Besides, she doesn't go that deep. Something must have happened," Phil reasoned.

"She is never stepping an inch close to that river," Annalise said with a tone of finality and evident fury.

"Don't be too harsh on her. Let's wait for her to wake up, and then she can explain to us what happened," Phil said as he wiped the tears dropping from Annalise's eyes.

"It's okay. Don't worry. Lucinda is safe. That's the most important thing for now," Phil said and hugged his wife.

Later in the evening, as Annalise was preparing dinner, she dished out a portion for her husband and daughter. She sat on the edge of the thinned foam as Lucinda opened her eyes and called out her name.

"Annalise!" Lucinda spoke with a faint smile.

Whenever she wanted her mom to smile, she called her by her name.

"Lucinda, how are you doing?" Annalise asked, smiling.

"I'm fine. Why are you crying, Mom?" Lucinda asked.

"I thought something bad might have happened to you. Why did you go deep into the water, knowing full well that you can't swim? What if we didn't get there on time? It could have been fatal. You know I can't survive the trauma of losing you, Lucinda," Annalise said.

"I was only trying to rescue this baby bird that fell into the water. Its wings were broken. I'm sorry I hurt myself while trying to save another life," Lucinda apologized.

"Don't worry, okay? I prepared something special for you. You will love it," Annalise said, smiling and patting Lucinda on the shoulder.

"Are you still upset with me?" Lucinda asked.

"Yes, I am upset with you but I understand that you were trying to save a life. So, cheer up," Annalise said.

Annalise helped her daughter up as she ran a water bath for her, after which she helped Lucinda put on her nightwear and fed her quietly.

Nothing in this world mattered to Annalise except Lucinda and Phil, her two most priceless possessions.

∞ ∞ ∞

Chapter 2

Lucinda slowly opened her eyes

Lucinda slowly opened her eyes to the dim sunray coming through the windows. She then stood up and walked towards the window, parting the curtains to let in the whole entrails of the sun. Having done that, she walked out of her room and went straight to her parent's bedroom, and on getting there, she quietly entered the room, seeing her mom was still fast asleep. Her dad had left very early in the morning. She walked to the window and opened the curtains to wake her mom.

"Good morning, Mom," Lucinda said, smiling.

Annalise slowly opened her eyes as she saw Lucinda sitting on the bed with her. Annalise got up slowly and took in her daughter, sitting down on the edge of the bed.

Lucinda would always wake up early, but she rarely came to her parent's room that early. She would instead go straight to the river to stay all alone.

"Lucinda," Annalise called.

"Yes, Mom. How are you, Annalise?" Lucinda asked, grinning.

"What are you doing in my room? You usually go the river because that's where you go every morning, but you're still here," Annalise observed.

"You asked me not to swim, and you even warned me never to go near the river again so that I won't drown," Lucinda replied.

"What are you up to, young lady? How can I help you? In fact, what do you want?" Annalise asked, now wide awake.

"Thanks for asking. I want to pay a visit to Grandma and Grandpa up on the mountain. You've told me so much about them. I woke up this morning desiring to see them. Can you take me there?" Lucinda pleaded, pouting her lips.

"Lucinda!" Annalise called.

"Mom, please, I haven't asked for anything for God knows how long now, and today I'm making this request. Please don't tell me you won't grant me this request. I beg of you, Mom," Lucinda replied.

"Alright, I have heard you, young lady. I will take you there to spend some time with them. Maybe after two weeks, come back home," Annalise said.

"Just two weeks?" Lucinda asked, raising her eyebrows.

"Yes, young lady, two weeks. Is there any problem?" Annalise asked.

"But what will I be doing if I come back home? Nothing! So, I feel it is best if I stayed there for at least a month." Lucinda replied.

"Leave my room now," Annalise said, pointing at the door, as Lucinda laughed and ran out.

Lucinda never took things seriously. She was always joking about everything, but she was fun to be with. Annalise didn't want her daughter to be far away from her. Although being the very playful and sometimes mischievous type, she always kept her company, although she had often made her talk too much. No doubt Annalise knew she would miss her daughter once she left for her parent's house.

As soon as Lucinda left, Annalise stood up and walked to the bathroom to have her bath. She didn't bother about preparing anything because nothing was at home, and that was the major reason her husband left very early in the morning to look for something they could eat for breakfast.

Annalise finished her bath and dressed up. Then she walked out of the room, meeting Lucinda sitting on the balcony.

"Lucinda, what are you doing outside?" Annalise asked.

"Nothing, just want to stay outside. Sit with me. Let's admire this beautiful natural scenery before us," Lucinda pleaded as Annalise came and sat down close to her.

"Mom, I'm hungry," Lucinda said after a few minutes of silence between the two filial friends.

"I know, just wait a little more. Your dad went to the farm, and he would branch out to the village market to get things before returning home. Once he is back, I will fix something for breakfast, okay?" Annalise said, patting her daughter on the back.

"Alright. So, while we wait for Dad to come back home, do you mind telling me a story?" Lucinda asked.

"What do you want me to tell you?" Annalise asked her daughter.

"I want to know more about your family, Mom. Why do my grandparents live on the mountain? Do they have neighbors?" Lucinda asked.

"Well, my parents lived on the mountain because of the calmness in that area, and nope, they don't have neighbors. I know the next question would be, how do they eat? Well, they travel to the village close to them to get foodstuffs every Friday. That's all," Annalise replied.

"Wow, that's nice," Lucinda said as she looked up, seeing her father coming back.

"That's Dad. He is coming home," Lucinda said as she ran towards her father and hugged him. She collected the hoe and cutlass her father was carrying and took them inside to keep behind the kitchen door. Lucinda then went back inside her parent's room and met her father sitting on the wooden chair. She went closer to him and sat on the floor.

"Dad, how are you doing?" Lucinda asked.

"I'm fine, and how about you?" Phil asked.

"I'm fine, Daddy, just hungry," Lucinda replied.

"Don't worry. Your mom is about to fix up something for breakfast. Wouldn't you like to join her?" Phil asked.

"I will, but Daddy, I need your help," Lucinda asked.

"My help? Well, anything for my daughter. So, tell me, how can Daddy help you?" Phil asked.

"Can you convince Mom to take me to the mountain so I can visit Grandma and Grandpa? You know I've never been there, and I have this intense desire to see them. I promise after a month; I will be back," Lucinda replied.

"Is that all you want?" Phil asked.

"Yes, Daddy," Lucinda replied.

"Alright. I will do that, but I don't think Mommy will let you stay for a month. Don't worry. You will go," Phil said.

"Thanks, Dad," Lucinda replied, smiling and getting up, ready to leave the room for the kitchen.

"You're welcome," Phil replied.

"I'm off to the kitchen to help Mom," Lucinda said and walked out of the room into the kitchen.

When Annalise was through with the preparation, she dished out her husband's own and handed the dish over to Lucinda to set down on the table in the sitting room while telling her she was coming out shortly to meet them. Lucinda obeyed and walked out with the food. Annalise soon followed her with two plates inside a tray—one for herself and the other for Lucinda.

"Food is ready," Lucinda announced as her father smiled and shifted the chair close to the center table. Annalise and Lucinda sat down as they said a quick prayer before digging into their food.

"So, Mom, when are you taking your little angel to Grandpa and Grandma?" Lucinda asked.

"Lucinda, you don't talk while eating." Annalise chided.

"Daddy, won't you talk to Mom; she won't allow me to visit Grannies." Lucinda protested in between a munch of food in her mouth.

"Anna, don't you think this is a nice idea? Staying alone at home might tempt her into going close to the river. You remember what happened the last time she did so, and mind you; it's about time she visited them. I think it's nice you take her on a visit to the mountain ranges so that she can spend some quality time with them, even if it is for two weeks or a month," Phil said.

"Two weeks is too short. How do you want me to spend some quality time with them in just two weeks?" Lucinda asked

"Lucinda, it's not that I don't want you to go. It's just that you are too stubborn. You're my daughter, and I'm your mother, and I tell you, you're very stubborn. You will visit my parents, and by the time you get there, you will start disturbing them and making outrageous demands." Annalise said.

"Aww! This isn't fair, Mom. How can you say your little angel is stubborn? I'm doubting whether I am still your little angel," Lucinda said, looking away.

"Hahaha! Remind me how old you are again.?" Annalise asked her daughter.

"Ten, Mom," Lucinda replied, folding her hands.

"You're her mother," Phil chipped in.

"Oh yes, I know. It's just that she talks like she is an adult," Annalise replied.

"So, when are you taking her to your parents?" Phil asked.

"Yes, Mom. When are you taking me to your parents?" Lucinda asked, smiling.

"I haven't even accepted yet. You two are just the same, no difference," Annalise said, sighing.

"We're waiting for an answer, Mom; when?" Lucinda asked.

"Alright, I'll be taking you there by this weekend," Annalise replied.

"Aww! That's so sweet of you, Mom. One kiss for you," Lucinda said, blowing a kiss to her parents, one after the other.

"You both are the best," Lucinda said, smiling as she continued with her food. Phil and Annalise looked at their daughter and smiled back.

Lucinda was one hell of a child, very stubborn and intelligent as well. Aside from that, she was lovely, such that one can mistake her for a goddess. Her skin was as fair as snow and her hair so black, with her blue eyes and pink lips. Lucinda shared the exact resemblance with her mother, but one thing that confused Annalise most times about her daughter was how she acted and behaved like an adult though she was just ten.

When they finished eating their food, Lucinda took the plates to the kitchen to wash. Then she retired to her bedroom to sleep. As Lucinda lay on the bed, she silently prayed that Friday would come quickly. And soon, it was Friday.

That morning, Lucinda was the first to wake up as she walked to her parent's room and knocked on the door. Her mom quickly rushed out, thinking something was wrong.

"Lucinda, what's the problem? It's only 6 a.m. Did you have a nightmare?" Annalise asked, looking surprised.

"Nightmare? That's the opposite of what I came here to say," Lucinda said, staring at her mom.

"So, what's the problem?" Annalise asked.

"I woke you up to let you know that today is Friday. Start preparing because I'm about to take my bath now," Lucinda said and walked out.

Annalise stood at the door looking at her daughter, wondering whether she was the one who gave birth to Lucinda. Quietly she went inside as Phil grinned, having heard what Lucinda said.

"Your daughter is so unbelievable," Annalise said. "How do you mean?" Phil asked.

"Can you imagine she woke me up so I can get ready to take her to the mountain ranges?" Annalise replied as Phil burst into quakes of laughter.

"What's funny?" Annalise asked, feeling surprised.

"She is your replica. So, anything she does now shouldn't surprise you at all. She is her mother's daughter." Phil said as Annalise frowned and walked out of the room.

Annalise walked straight into her daughter's room to help her sort out the clothes she would travel with.

"Mom, I thought you were going to get me some new clothes?" Lucinda asked.

"Lucinda, you know I don't have the money now. Don't worry; I would get you something better soon, okay?" Annalise assured.

Lucinda hugged her mother and whispered into her ears: "I was only joking with you. You don't have to feel bad about not getting me new clothes. We already have a roof over our heads, and we have something to eat. I'm grateful for that. So, smile, Mommy. Don't worry. In the future, I would get you all the finer things of life and would take you to the city."

Lucinda smiled and walked out of the room as Annalise wiped the tears that trickled down her cheeks. She looked up and said, "God, thank you for giving me a daughter like Lucinda." She then placed everything in the backpack and zipped it up.

Annalise prepared breakfast, so they could all have something to eat. Phil bade them goodbye as he went to the farm. Annalise held Lucinda's bag, and together they went off.

****

"Who could that be?" Maya said as she stood up to check who was knocking at the door.

"Are you expecting anyone?" Greg asked.

"Of course not," Maya replied and opened the door to see her daughter and granddaughter grinning as she opened her arms to hug them both with so much excitement.

"Who do we have here?" Greg said, standing up as her daughter Annalise hugged him.

"I missed you so much, Mother," Annalisa said, grinning.

"I missed you too, Anna beloved," Maya replied, pecking her Annalisa on the cheek.

"And who do you have with you?" Maya asked, looking at Annalisa.

"My daughter, Lucinda, of course. Hahaha! Have you forgotten her? It's been a long time since you saw her. I think you saw her last when she was four. She wouldn't let me rest unless I bring here. You know Lucinda and how stubborn she can be. I had to bring her here," Annalise replied.

"You did well. We missed her too, and we have been planning to visit again. Who would have known that my granddaughter was missing us as well? Aww!" Maya said.

"Don't worry, Granny. I will spend a lot of time here with you, okay?" Lucinda said as she smiled.

"Exactly, just as I wished, now that you're grown up. At least we are going to have good company," said Maya.

"Yea, Grandma!" Lucinda almost shouted at the approval of her grandmother. They all sat down inside the parlor made up of mainly wooden furniture, with no modern gadgets. It was a small house with four rooms: one bedroom, one kitchen, one store, and a parlor. Inside the parlor where they all sat was an enormous couch, with very soft foam padding all around the wood.

A more miniature replica of it was situated opposite it, and the door to the parlor opened in between. Behind the colossal couch was a wooden table, chocolate. And there were brownish curtains over the parlor's three windows, with a thick brown rug covering the entire wooden floor.

Here and there were sundry domestic Chinese utensils—contoured and chiseled flower vases, fresh flowers, a fireplace for warmth. Lucinda found the setting cozy. Her mother had thought the place would seem out of place for her. What held a unique attraction for Lucinda was the forest ambiance of the abode.

The house was located amid a forest upon a mountain, away from civilization. There was no threat of wild animals in sight.

As they all sat down talking, Maya walked into the kitchen and dished out food for her daughter and granddaughter, and while eating, they touched upon sundry subjects.

Later on, Lucinda became busy with her grandpa, teaching her a traditional Chinese game Lucinda saw for the first time. Later that evening, Annalise informed them she was about to leave.

After hugging her parents, she went straight to where Lucinda was sitting alone, on the smaller couch, and hugged her, whispering into her ears: "Please don't disturb my parents and better behave yourself."

Lucinda stole a glance at her and smiled.

"Trust me, Annalise; I will be a good girl," Lucinda said, still smiling as Annalise laughed, her laughter triggered by the way Lucinda used to call her by her name.

"Take care of yourself," Annalise said as she opened the door and journeyed back home.

∞∞∞

Chapter 3

But, Granny, I don't want to go home

B ut Granny, I don't want to go home yet. Mom isn't even here to pick me up, so why do you want me to go home now?" Lucinda asked dejectedly.

Her grandmother had spoken to her about going back home, but it was apparent Lucinda wasn't taking that. The two weeks her mother gave had elapsed, and Maya needed to take her home.

"Your mom isn't here to pick you up because I will be the one taking you home," Maya said.

"Are you pushing me away from your house? I thought I was your granddaughter, or don't you enjoy my company?" Lucinda asked, folding her hands and looking at Maya disapprovingly.

"I enjoy your company, honey, but your mom's instruction should be obeyed," Maya replied.

"What's going on here?" Greg asked as he walked into the parlor from one of his many explorations of the woods—something that gave him holy joy.

"Thank God Grandpa is back. Grandpa, do you know Grandma wants to take me back home? I have asked her if I did anything wrong so I can apologize, but she said no. She wants to take me home, which means she

17

doesn't love and enjoy my company anymore." Lucinda said, almost on the verge of crying.

"Oh, little one, don't mind your grandma. She loves you, sure. We both love you so much. Grandma is taking you home. Your mom and dad miss you a lot. She is taking you home so you can spend some time with them, and before you know it, you will be back here again," Greg said.

"Why is it that I don't believe you both?" Lucinda asked, placing her hands on her waist, standing akimbo.

"Has Grandpa ever lied to you before?" Greg asked, clearly flustered.

"Nope, you haven't, but I'm not having a good feeling about this. You both are trying to trick me into going back home, which is not fair. Going back home, I won't have the chance to do anything, like exploring the woods with you or going down to the river in the valley. Back home, Mom and Dad banned me from going close to the river. And when I'm there, I will be home alone most of the time with no one to talk to.

I wish I have a playmate or even a pet," Lucinda said and ran off into the lone room in the house with tears in her eyes.

"Indeed, Annalise gave birth to her replica. She acted like her when she was her age, yet she acts like an adult and reasons like one. Wow," Greg said as he sat on the oversized couch.

"You know we have to take her back home. Annalise can't stay a month without seeing her daughter. And even if we don't take her home, Annalise will surely be here in few days to take her home, anyway," Maya whispered.

"Don't worry. I will convince her to go home with you; leave that to me," Greg whispered back, smiling.

"That sounds good. So, when will you talk to her?" Maya asked.

"This evening. Then tomorrow, you will take her home," Greg replied.

"That's nice," Maya said as she walked into the room.

That evening, Greg had walked into the room and met Lucinda sitting down and staring out from the window into the woods.

"Are you still angry with your Grandpa?" Greg asked as he sat close to Lucinda.

"I'm not angry with you as you did nothing wrong," Lucinda said with her eyes still staring out the window.

"I doubt it because you're not even looking at me, which shows you are still angry with me. Can you forgive me, my little angel?" Greg asked.

"Why do you want me to go home?" Lucinda asked.

"Because...," Greg was talking when Lucinda interjected.

"Don't lie to me, Grandpa. I'm not a baby," Lucinda said.

"You're just ten years old," Greg replied, smiling.

"Grandpa!" Lucinda exclaimed slowly.

"Alright, I'm sorry. The way you were missing us back then, even without ever meeting or knowing us then, is the same way your parents are missing you now. My dear, you see, that's the main reason you have to go home." Greg said.

"You will come back and pick me up, right? Lucinda asked with eyes wide open in anticipation.

"I will, dear," Greg replied.

"Is that a promise?" Lucinda asked.

"Of course, it is," Greg replied, smiling.

"It's not that I'm missing home, but if I go home, I won't be allowed to go close to the river. That's the only place I go to play, the only place I feel at peace, that even I cannot explain," Lucinda said.

"What could be the attraction in the river for that you go there to play every day?" Greg asked.

"Well, I've not told anyone this, but sometimes in the morning, I get to find beautiful Seashell washed ashore, and they are all beautiful. I can't get to bring them home, so I always hid them close to the riverbed," Lucinda said, smiling.

"That's nice but don't worry, for once you meet with your mom, stay with her for some time, you will come back here, and I promise you, we will go hunting," Greg said.

"You're not joking, right?" Lucinda asked, beaming with smiles.

"I'm serious, Lucy," Greg replied as he hugged his granddaughter.

"So, are you the one taking me home, or will Grandma do that?" Lucinda asked.

"Grandma will do that," Greg replied.

"Alright, let's eat," Lucinda said as she stood up, and together she walked out with her grandpa. They had their dinner that night, and they all retired to bed, the two Grannies on one bed, while Lucinda slept on a spare bed inside the same room. It was a large room.

The next day, Maya woke Lucinda up as she helped arrange Lucinda's clothes while Lucinda has her bath. Maya finished up and went out to have her bath. When she was through, she had to fix something for breakfast, although Lucinda claimed she wasn't hungry. Around 9 a.m., they both journeyed back home, with Lucinda asking her grandmother several questions.

In a few hours, they were home, and Lucinda was eager to rush inside to see her mom. She touched the door handle, and luckily it wasn't locked. She pushed it opened, and they both walked inside. Lucinda screamed her mom's name and her dad's name as they both rushed out and hugged her tightly.

"Mom, please try not to kill me. I was only gone for two weeks," Lucinda said, smiling.

"I know. I missed you so much. I had already told your dad that if my mother didn't bring you home today, I will come there myself tomorrow and bring you back home." Annalise said, smiling.

"You both are only engrossed in your daughter that you did not even notice my presence," Maya said as Phil walked closer to her and hugged her.

"We're so sorry. It's just that we have missed her so much. Annalise won't stop talking about her since last night," Phil said, smiling.

"She is obsessed with her daughter, Lucinda. I'm so not surprised," Maya replied as she sat down, watching Annalise and her daughter.

Lucinda dropped her backpack while Annalise went inside to get something for her mother to drink.

"Why didn't Father come with you?" Phil asked as he sat next to Maya.

"He is busy, my dear, as always with the nature surrounding us. But don't worry, the next visit, we both are coming together," Maya replied.

"That sounds great," Phil said.

"So, Mom, here is your tea," Annalise said as she handed the teacup over to her mom.

"Thank you so much," Maya replied as she sipped at the tea while grinning.

"Just like always, you're good with this," Maya commended.

"Mommy, I hope this drama queen didn't create a scene for you over there?" Annalise asked.

"You gave birth to her, and I'm happy you know she is a drama queen, but all the same, we enjoyed her company. Your father is coming to pick her up in two weeks. He made that promise to her." Maya replied.

"Oh! No problem then." Phil said as Annalise eyed him.

"Mommy, tell Dad to come over next month. I have missed him so much," Annalise pleaded.

"Maybe you should tell that to your father," Maya replied as she sipped her tea. They discussed other random stuff before Maya bade them goodbye and left for the mountains.

Lucinda had woken up that morning, but her parents weren't at home. And she wondered aloud: "Where could they be? They didn't even ask me to follow them." Quietly, she sat on her father's rocking chair. It was already getting close to three hours, and there was no sign of her parents, but she later ventured into the kitchen and found out her mother had left something for her to eat.

"Maybe they went to the farm, and probably they will go to the market to sell off some of the farm's produce," Lucinda soliloquized as she sat down on the chair and ate her food quietly. When she finished, she washed the plates and walked into her room. She didn't go close to the stream because of the incident that happened last time. She laid back on her bed and drifted off to sleep.

"Wake up, Lucy!" Annalise tapped her daughter as Lucinda slowly opened her eyes.

"Sorry, we didn't tell you we were leaving very early in the morning, and also, we are sorry for coming back late," Annalise apologized.

"No problem. I understand," Lucinda said, smiling.

"Let me fix up dinner; then I will let you know when it's ready," Annalise said. Lucinda smiled and watched her mother walk out of the room.

She stood up and walked into the bathroom, and poured the little water remaining in the bucket on her body. Then she dried her body and quickly wore her nightwear.

After a few minutes, Lucinda went to the kitchen to meet her mom. Annalise was already done with the food as she dished out Lucinda's portion and gave it to her. Lucinda ate quietly and returned to bed. To Annalise, her returning Lucinda was unusually quiet, unlike the vivacious Lucinda that she knew she gave birth to.

Annalise suspected maybe it was because they weren't home all day. She, however, quietly ate with her husband Phil before they both retired to bed.

∞∞∞

Chapter 4

On a particular morning

On a particular morning, some days after she returned from the mountain ranges, Lucinda woke up and quietly scampered into the kitchen to prepare breakfast for all of them. She didn't want to disturb her parents. She took the breakfast to her parents in their room. By the time she got there, they were already awake but discussing matters in low tones. There was an epidemic of flu spreading across the region, and so far, Lucinda was the only one out of the three members of this household who had not yet contracted it. Her parents were already down with the virus.

"Good morning, Mom. Good morning, Dad," Lucinda said as she dropped the tray of food on the table.

"Morning," Annalise replied.

"I prepared breakfast so we can eat," Lucinda announced.

"What a surprise! You're just ten, Lucinda," Phil said, more out of curiosity.

"I'm ten, but I normally stay with Mom in the kitchen. Although she hasn't allowed me to prepare anything, I've done it today; it's left for you to decide on the taste's goodness. Now that Mom was down, I'll have to step in," Lucinda replied.

23

"Lucinda, I want you to promise Mom and Dad something and just say yes when I tell you this," Annalise said weakly.

"I will always say yes, anything for you both to get healed and be back on your feet," Lucinda replied.

"Listen, Lucinda, this illness is spreading everywhere, and it's so contagious. I want you to go back to my parent's place, so you don't get infected. If we get healed somehow, then we will come back for you. Staying here with us and cleaning us up increases the chances of you getting infected," Annalise said.

"You want me to stay with Grandpa and Grandma? What will happen to you both? Who will take care of you, cook for you and fetch water from the river for both of you? Who will keep it clean? No one. Mom, you still need me around to do all these," Lucinda said.

"We can cope on our own. Just go, Lucinda. I trust you. You're smart enough, and know your way up there. Just leave, please," Phil said.

"I'm not going anywhere without you both. I don't care if I get infected or not. You both are my parents. I don't want to go anywhere without you both by my side. Please don't ask me to leave," Lucinda said as tears trickled down her eyes.

"We both want you to go now, Lucinda, for your safety because we love you and want you to stay alive. Please, dear," Annalise said.

"Can we talk about this later?" Lucinda said as she took out a spoon and started feeding her parents. She took the plates to the kitchen to wash. Soon after, she left the house and headed down to the river. And on getting to the riverbank, she sat down quietly and later started soliloquizing.

"Mom and Dad want me to leave them. They want me to go up to the mountain and stay with my grandparents, but I'm going nowhere. How will they be able to cope without me? Have they thought of that? Who will do things for them? I'm not scared of getting infected. I just want us all to be together. If they die, I die with them. If they live, I live with them," Lucinda said to herself as she threw pebbles into the river. She stayed there meditating on sundry issues, gathering Seashells, observing the river's flow, and watching fishes darting here and there.

She didn't even know when the sun rose to the sky, and when it dawned on her, it was time to head back home.

When she got home, she saw her parents were asleep. As she walked to her room, she laid back on her foam mattress and slept off herself.

She later woke up in the evening and checked her parents to see that they were still asleep.

"This is unusual. Mom and Dad have been sleeping since morning now. Well, let me leave them alone," Lucinda muttered to herself as she went to the kitchen to prepare something for dinner, after which she ate her portion and kept the remaining one for her parents.

She then walked back to her room and knelt to pray, saying, "Dear God, if you can hear me, heal my parents. I want nothing to happen to them. I know this illness is slowly wiping out everyone in the village, and no one was being spared.

Please, Lord, do this for me. I need my parents now more than ever. I can't do anything without them. They are my life, and I'm their life. I miss everything about Mom and how she scolds me, and the way she laughs. But today, she is struggling to even talk to me, same with my dear father. This illness has stolen the joy in our family. Please, Lord, return my prayer by healing my parents. Amen." After prayers, she stood up and laid back down on her bed to sleep.

****

In the morning, Lucinda yawned as she opened her eyes. She then stood up and opened the window curtains to see that the sun was already up. She walked out of the room and went straight to her parent's room as she tapped them to wake up, having been disgusted with their unusual sleep.

"Mom, Dad, please wake up," Lucinda said as she tapped her parents, but there was not even a whimper of movement from them as their bodies laid there like a log of wood and stone-cold as frozen beef. Frightened, Lucinda placed her ear close to her mom's heart, only to discover there was no sign of beating. She became more frightened as she did the same to her father. Her fright turned to hysteria.

"Mom, Dad, you promised you were not going anywhere. Please wake up!" Lucinda shouted with tears in her eyes.

"Please wake up. I prayed to God to heal you. I didn't tell him to take my parents away from me. Please wake up. I promise to do anything you want. Just wake up!" Lucinda yelled as she kept touching her parents, hoping that one of them would open their eyes, but nothing happened.

She ran out of the house and headed straight for the mountain which took hours before she could get there.

"Who could bang at the door like that?" Maya asked as she stood up to check who it was. She was surprised when she saw Lucinda barefooted and looking fatigued.

"What's wrong with you?" Greg asked as he came out of the room.

Lucinda sat still and was crying.

"Who is after you? Talk to me, Lucinda. What's the problem? What about your mom and dad? Where are they?" Maya kept on with her barrage of questions.

"Mom and Dad, they left without me," Lucinda replied in between tears.

"How do you mean? I don't understand," Greg asked.

"They were sick. Everyone in the village is down with this illness, including Mom and Dad. Yesterday morning, they pleaded with me to come here and stay with you for a while, but I refused, telling them they needed me to be around them. And this morning, I woke up to feed them, but they wouldn't answer me. Their body was so cold. They had promised me they would not go anywhere without me," Lucinda said.

"Are you saying that Annalise and Phil are dead?" Greg asked with trembling lips.

Lucinda nodded with tears in her eyes.

"This can't be happening," Maya said as she held her granddaughter tightly, but Lucinda kept mentioning her parent's names until she was sleeping.

"They were sick, and they didn't let anyone know. Now her parents are gone. The last time I saw my daughter was when I went to take Lucinda back home. Death cheated me big time.

I didn't see my daughter one last time before she went on this journey. Annalise and Phil, you both should have waited a little longer. How will Lucinda cope without you two?" Maya asked as she wiped the tears from her cheeks.

"Although I felt something was wrong with me, I didn't know that my daughter and her husband were dying. If I knew, I would have brought them here and treated them with natural herbs.

I never got the chance to see Phil for some years now." Greg lamented bitterly.

"We can't leave the bodies there. We have to burn them and keep the ashes for Lucinda, their daughter." Maya said.

"Stay back, dear. I know how to do this! I'll be back before night falls," Greg said to Maya, who was still lamenting bitterly as she sat on the smaller couch.

"Take care of yourself and when you see Annalise and Phil, tell them we miss them," Maya said as Greg was leaving the house.

Greg nodded as he stood up and walked outside. He took the horse and raced down to the village.

He got to the house where his daughter lived with her husband. As he came down and tied the horse to the tree, he walked inside slowly and met his daughter and Phil, just the way Lucinda had left them.

"You would have sent a message to me. Somehow Annalise, and I know you won't be dead because I would have tried everything humanly possible to heal you. Your child is in tears. She keeps saying that you both left without her. You made so many promises to her, and you didn't keep any. She yearns for both of you," Greg was saying in between sobs, slowly but surely grieving.

Gradually he could pull the two bodies out of the house. He laid them on the woods and poured oil on them before setting them ablaze.

"Dust we are from and to dust, we shall return," Greg said as he poured the ashes into the bottle which he had come with.

He climbed onto his horse and jogged back to the mountain top. He was in pain even though he refused to show it.

****

"Grandma, are my parents ever going to come back home?" Lucinda asked with tears in her eyes. She had woken up and kept bombarding Maya with questions concerning her parents.

"They will come home, but not soon," Maya replied. She felt terrible as she couldn't believe she had lied to her granddaughter.

"What of Grandpa? Where is he?" Lucinda asked.

"Oh, he went out to sort out some things. He will be back any moment from now," Maya replied.

"So, should I dish out your food now for you to eat?" Maya added.

"When Mom and Dad come back home, I will eat. You said they are coming back home, right? That's not a problem. I will wait for them," Lucinda said with her hand holding her chin.

"I'm home," Greg said as he walked into the room.

"Grandpa. Grandma said my parents would be back home, so I'm waiting for them," Lucinda said, sitting up.

"Here, have this," Greg said as he gave a silver bottle to Lucinda.

"What's this?" Lucinda asked.

"It's a gift from your parents. They want you to keep it, and please don't misplace it," Greg said.

"A gift from my parents? Where are they?" Lucinda said, standing up as she ran outside. She came back a few minutes later and looked at her grandparent's askance and said, " I checked everywhere, but I couldn't see them. Where are they?"

"Lucy, listen, your mom dend dad gave me this to keep for you a long time ago. I want you to have it because you are of age," Greg lied.

"Why do I feel no one is telling me the truth here? Where are my mom and dad?" Lucinda asked with tears in her eyes.

"They want you to have this in memory of them. They might not come home soon," Greg replied.

"That's not fair. They promised they were going to go everywhere with me. They made that promise to me. Even if Mom would leave me behind, I trust my dad. I'm his little princess.

He makes sure I'm happy every day. He says yes to everything I want to do. You can't just tell me that my parents aren't coming home soon. I need them now. Get them for me. I want to go with them," Lucinda screamed as Maya hugged her tightly, patting her on the back.

"Granny, I want them home," Lucinda cried the more amidst tears.

"They aren't deaf to your cries, and please, trust me, Lucinda. Your parents are coming back," Maya replied.

The atmosphere was awkward for Greg. He cast a furtive glance at them and walked out. He had cremated his daughter and son-in-law. If anyone had told him his daughter would be dead this day, he wouldn't believe that person. He reasoned that death had played a fast one on them.

∞ ∞ ∞

Chapter 5

Greg and Maya had tried all they could

Greg and Maya had tried all they could to make Lucinda leave the room, but all to no avail. She wouldn't budge and rarely touched the food. In the morning, Maya and Greg woke up and sat down on their bed, waiting for Lucinda to wake up too. They had agreed to talk sense to her.

Soon after, Lucinda stirred and opened her eyes and had them focused on the wall. Maya wiped the tears that had gathered in her eyes that early morning. She was unable to sleep in the night.

The death of Annalise and her husband had been traumatic to her and Greg too. But like a man, Greg carried himself with the calmness of the situation required. Maya was still wallowing in pain, sadness, and fear, the fear of losing Lucinda too.

They waited for Lucinda to become fully awake before they ventured into talking to her.

"Lucinda, how are you feeling now? I hope you slept well?" Maya said.

"Yes, thank you, Grandma," Lucinda replied without moving her eyes an inch off the wall.

"Lucinda, my dear, you're hurting yourself, and you're also hurting us. Had your mom been here, she wouldn't want to see you like this. You

30

can't continue like this forever. Cheer up, my dear, and then we will go out and have some fun together," Greg said.

"If hurting myself would bring back my parents, then I'm willing to hurt myself until eternity. They didn't deserve this kind of cruelty. We lived far away from the village, yet somehow, they contracted the disease. Mom and Dad suffered so much.

Why didn't nature spare them? I need the love of my parents. I wanted them to be around me. I just want my mom and dad home," Lucinda replied as tears started rushing down her cheeks.

"We also want them home, but it had happened. Death is the only thing we humans have no power over. The least we can do is to respect their last wishes, and you are yet to tell us the last thing your parents told you before their death," Maya said.

"They said nothing! Nothing!" Lucinda replied and burst out crying.

"It's alright, child. Please stop. Please." Greg begged.

"You know Mom and Dad requested for nothing; They only wanted me far away so I wouldn't contract the disease. Every day I prayed to the creator to heal my parents. I wanted a miracle. I cried and pleaded, but it's obvious it fell on deaf ears.

The day they died, I had woken up in the morning to cook for them as usual, only to meet their lifeless bodies. Mom, if you can hear me, know that you hurt me so much. Remember, you promised you would stay with me until the end of time, but you were quick to leave after spending a decade with me.

Why couldn't you both defy death to be with me?" Lucinda yelled as Greg got up from the bed to hold her tightly, consoling her.

Maya left the room quickly with tears in her eyes as she walked into the parlor. She sat on the oversized couch crying. She took out an old wooden box, opened it up, and took out the Seashell there as she ran her hands over it with tears dripping on it.

Greg walked into the parlor after a few minutes to meet Maya holding the ancestral Seashell.

"What of Lucinda?" Maya asked.

"I've been able to put her back to sleep. Why are you holding the Seashell?" Greg asked.

"Well, this has been passed from generation to generation, and I know it must have cost a fortune. I don't mind selling it to give Lucinda the good life she deserves. I want to take her somewhere far away. It hurts to see her going through so much pain at such tender age," Maya said.

"Taking her far away isn't what she needs right now. She only wants her parents back, and we know it is impossible, but I hope sooner she will let go of this terrible thing," Greg said.

"Annalise, why did you have to go? Can't you just come back somehow? I don't know how, but please, your daughter needs you." Maya said amidst tears, which dripped down her cheeks and dropped on the Seashell.

Greg took the Seashell from Maya and placed it back inside the box so he could be able to console her.

"You don't have to cry. I know you. Annalise and Lucinda share the same quality. Console yourself in Lucinda, please, my dear. You are so emotional right now, but please be strong for your grandchild. She needs you. She needs us." Greg said as he hugged his wife.

Lucinda later woke up before noon but refused to get up from her bed and refused every request to eat any food. In the evening, she got up from the bed, seeing an old picture of her parents hanging on the wall. She took it down and smiled, but the smiling quickly replaced with tears.

"I miss you, Annalise and Phil. I want you both to come home. I want to see that smile on your face whenever I call you by your first name, Mom.

I miss all the fun we had together. It's fun staying with Grandma and Grandpa, but I wouldn't trade you both for anything else in this world. Mom and Dad, why didn't you both stay for a long time? Why would you have to leave now?

I wish I can turn back the hands of the clock so we all could come here. If only you both listened to me, maybe you both wouldn't have contracted the disease, and you will be safe with me. I wish I tried harder in convincing you both to come here. I wish I tried harder." Lucinda said, wiping her tears with the back of her hand as she dropped the picture on the wooden floor.

Lucinda stood up and walked towards the window. She slowly opened the curtain, and after standing there for close to thirty minutes, she strolled back to her bed. When she heard her name, she turned around and looked but saw no one. She closed the window and shifted back the curtains as she walked out of the room.

"Grandma!" Lucinda called as she got to the sitting room. Maya rushed out of the kitchen as soon as she heard Lucinda's voice.

"Lucinda, you came out from the room?" Maya asked, feeling surprised and happy.

"Yeah, where is Grandpa?" Lucinda asked.

"He just stepped outside now. I think he will back in a few minutes," Maya replied.

"Alright," Lucinda said as she turned to go back to her room.

"Lucinda!" Maya called.

"Yes, Granny," Lucinda answered as she turned back.

"Why don't you sit here, please? Don't go back to bed now, please. You've been there since morning. You can sit in the parlor," Maya pleaded.

"But you're busy in the kitchen; who will be with me in the parlor?" Lucinda asked.

"I'm here with you. I'm not all that busy." Maya lied as she watched Lucinda sit down on the wooden chair beside the cooking stove. Maya heaved a sigh of relief as she sat down too. She was happy that finally, Lucinda had come to terms with the reality of losing her parents to death.

"So, what will you like us to do?" Maya asked.

"Of all the places in the world, why did you choose this mountain?" Lucinda asked with her hands on her chin.

"Because this place is quiet and heavenly. There is no disturbance. The tranquility of the environment gives us innermost peace," Maya replied, smiling.

"My mom, your daughter, did she ever like here? She had no one to play with," Lucinda asked.

"Annalise, your mother is a gift from God. She was unique. She was the main reason we chose here because she values calmness more than anything else, and that was the main reason you and your parents lived close to the riverside. Annalise wasn't the type who had many friends.

She made friends with the animals. When she got married and moved away, I felt pain. My daughter is my most priceless possession. She is gone, but I'm happy you are here," Maya said, trying hard not to cry.

"You know it's okay to let those tears out. That's what my mom taught me. That way, you will feel a lot better," Lucinda said as Maya stared at her. She was surprised this was coming from a ten-year-old girl.

"Lucinda, you"

"I act like an adult, I know. Mom says that to me a lot. Anytime I cry, don't stop me. I'm only letting out my emotions. Having it stuck right there in me can lead to something worse for me. I miss my parents, and they are worth every single tear I shed for their demise. So, I understand when you cry because of your daughter, Annalise, and her husband, Phil. They deserve every bit of tears; they are worth it," Lucinda said.

"You know I miss her so much, and, I'm scared; I want nothing bad to happen to you. Please, Lucinda, don't stay in your bed alone tomorrow. Try to come out like you did this evening. It hurts me so much that you're doing this to yourself," Maya said.

"I'm sorry if I was hurting myself, but I promise not to hurt myself again. Do you know why?" Lucinda asked.

"No, I don't, but why, if I may ask?" Maya said.

"Because my parents are back home. I heard their voice, and I can feel their presence," Lucinda said, smiling.

Maya was shocked when she heard that as she curiously looked at Lucinda.

"I'm not mad, Granny. I know what I'm saying; my parents are back," Lucinda said as she stood up and walked back into the room.

Maya placed her hand on her chin as she looked at the receding figure of her granddaughter.

"Please heal my granddaughter of this pain. She is too young and can't bear it anymore," She muttered to herself.

At that instant, Greg came inside and met Maya, lost in her thoughts.

"Maya!" Greg called, but to no response from Maya. He went and touched her as she jerked back to reality.

"Your body is here, but your mind is lost. What were you thinking about?" Greg asked as he sat down.

"Lucinda came out, and we talked," Maya replied.

"That's good news. Aside from that, why do you look lost?" Greg asked.

"Lucinda told me her parents are back, and she can feel their presence," Maya said.

"Wow! I wasn't expecting this," Greg said.

"I just hope she doesn't hurt herself. I'm scared of what she said. Talking about her dead parents being back is crazy," Maya said.

"Don't worry. I know Lucinda will overcome this. She is young, and anything happening now happened. She is young, and she will heal. Don't worry," Greg said as Maya smiled and walked back into the kitchen to fix dinner.

When Lucinda walked into the room, she laid down on the bed, and on looking up, she started talking: "I heard your voice today, Annalise. I heard when you called my name. That was your voice, Mom. I know you're back. I can remember what Granny said that you and Dad would be back, and you know what, I believed every word she said to me that day because I know my parents can't just leave without coming home to know how their little angel is doing. This past night without you–just one night - has been hell for me. Grandpa and Grandma have tried to console me, but I want you both home so we can live together as one happy family again," Lucinda said as she closed her eyes.

"Lucinda!" The voice called again.

Lucinda smiled and said: "I can hear you though I don't know where you are at the moment, trust me, I will find you."

∞∞∞

Chapter 6
On this fateful morning

On this fateful morning, Maya had prepared breakfast, and after dishing out Lucinda's portion, she left for the next village with Greg for an emergency. Something cropped up. Lucinda was still asleep when they left, but Maya placed the food where she could see it before leaving the house and making sure that the front door was locked properly.

Later in the morning, Lucinda woke up to discover that her grandparents were not in the room. She went out to the parlor, but they were not there, and then to the kitchen. It was there she realized she was alone in the house, and on looking around, she saw her food neatly kept for her on a kitchen table.

She stood there looking at the food and wondering where her grandparents could have gone. She, of course, knew that they must have gone out on an essential assignment; and that they didn't want to disturb her while she was still asleep.

"But where could they be? Where could they have gone?" Lucinda wondered aloud as she walked out of the kitchen back to the parlor. As she tried to open the front door, she discovered it was also locked from the outside. She then went out through the back door, opening it from inside.

When she stepped out, she went to the horse's stable by the house's side. Since her mourning period, she hadn't been there. On unlocking the stable door, she walked inside and saw the horses tied to the ground.

"Wow, they still look beautiful," Lucinda silently muttered as she ran her fingers over the body of the two horses.

"Do you have a name? What should I call you?" Lucinda asked.

"I will think of a name for you two," She said, smiling.

"I think I have to come here more often," She added as she turned and walked out.

"Lucinda!" The voice called again.

"This is surely my mother's voice. Where can I find you, Mom?" Lucinda said, looking around to see who called her name, but with no form of fear.

"Lucinda! I'm here," The voice said.

"Where are you?" Lucinda asked.

"What are you doing here?" Maya asked as she walked in.

"You and Grandpa weren't in, so I let myself out through the back door," Lucinda replied.

"And who were you talking to? I heard when you were asking where are you to the air?" Maya asked.

"My mom called my name, and she said she is in here," Lucinda replied.

Maya looked at her and then looked around before she said to Lucinda: "Your mother isn't here, Lucinda."

"If you came earlier, you would have heard when she called my name. I swear she is in here," Lucinda said.

Maya held Lucinda's hand and walked with her out of the stable. She locked it up correctly and walked inside with her.

"Lucinda dear, listen. No one called you. It's just that your imagination is playing tricks on you," Maya said."That's not true. I know what I heard, Granny. My mom is back here. I can hear her voice. It's not my fault if you can't hear her." Lucinda said amidst tears as she rushed into the room.

"God, what is happening?" Maya asked as she sat down on the chair inside the parlor.

"Is everything alright?" Greg asked as he walked in to meet Maya with her head bowed.

"Everything isn't okay. I'm scared. I don't know what is happening to Lucinda." Maya replied.

"How do you mean? Is she not okay?" Greg asked as he sat down.

"She is okay. I came back and figured out she wasn't in her room, but I could find her in the stable. Without her knowing I was behind her, I overheard her asking someone where she is.

I tried asking her who the person was, and she said it was her mom and that she is back. When I tried letting her know it was just a figment of her imagination playing tricks on her, she screamed and said, it's not my fault if I can't hear the voice. Then she ran inside the room. I fear for her. I'm scared of how she is acting. What could be wrong?" Maya asked.

"Maybe her imagination is indeed playing tricks on her," Greg said.

"But she wouldn't understand that, and she doesn't want to hear anything contrary to her thoughts," Maya replied, exasperated.

"Where is she?" Greg asked.

"Inside the room, of course. Where else?" Maya replied as Greg excused himself and walked into the room.

"Can I come in?" Greg asked as he stood at the door.

"Come in," Lucinda replied as Greg walked in and sat at the edge of the bed.

"You don't look okay. What's the problem, dear? Greg asked.

"I heard the voice. It was loud and clear. I know my mom is somewhere around here, and I have to find her," Lucinda replied.

"What voice are you talking about?" Greg asked.

"My parents are back. I know I heard that voice. Grandma won't believe me. She thinks it's my imagination playing tricks on me," Lucinda replied.

"How sure are you that your parents are back? And how come you're the only one who can hear this voice?" Greg asked calmly.

"I'm hundred percent sure, but I don't know why you can't hear the voice. It's not my fault," Lucinda replied.

"Listen, my angel. Your parents are not back. Even if they are coming back, not soon. Perhaps because you have been thinking so much about them, that's why you have heard their voices," Greg replied.

"Have I ever lied to you before?" Lucinda asked, eyes blazing.

"No, you haven't. Why do you ask?" Greg asked.

"So, why do you find it hard to believe me when I say that my parents are back? I heard the voice, and I know that's her voice. Nothing you would ever say or do that can make me believe my parents aren't back. Don't worry, Grandpa, eventually, you will find out on your own that my parents are back here indeed," Lucinda replied.

"Lucinda, my dear, I do not doubt you, but my problem is that you're the only one that hears the voice," Greg asked.

"I don't know, Grandpa. I can't know either," Lucinda replied.

"Alright, if you say so. I won't disturb you over this matter again," Greg said.

"Does that mean you now believe me?" Lucinda asked.

"Of course, I believe you," Greg said half grudgingly as he didn't want to stress the matter any further.

"Let me meet with your grandma. We have things to do," Greg said. "Alright, take care," Lucinda replied, smiling.

Greg stood up and walked out of the room when Lucinda called him and said: "Thank you for believing me," Greg smiled and walked out of the room.

He entered the kitchen to meet Maya slicing onions.

"Any luck?" Maya asked, still busy with her hands.

"No luck. Maybe her parents are back, and only she can hear the voices," Greg said, shrugging.

"Are you believing her?" Maya asked.

"Of course, I have no choice. This girl hasn't lied to both of us before. It isn't her imagination too, or her mind is playing tricks on her. She knows what she heard, and according to her, it's her parent's voice. Even if we can't hear them, the only thing we can do is to believe her. That's the only thing," Greg replied.

"But....."

"There are no buts in this case, Maya. Lucinda is already going through a lot. Her parents died right in her presence. At ten, she has gone through a lot, and you know Lucinda isn't someone who will wake up one morning to fabricate stories just to gain our attention. According to her, she heard a voice, and that voice belongs to her parents. The least we can do is to believe her, even if we can't hear the voice. But one thing is certain, Annalise and Phil are back, and their daughter only feels their presence," Greg replied. "But will Lucinda ever be okay?" Maya asked.

"Lucinda is more than okay. If she says anything, believe her. I beg of you. That's the only thing she wants from us," Greg replied.

"If you say so," Maya replied grudgingly.

"I will be in the stable. I need to check on the horses," Greg said and left immediately.

Maya finished cooking and dished out the food as she placed Lucinda's food on a tray and carried it to her.

"Thanks, Granny," Lucinda said, collecting the food from her.

"You're welcome," Maya replied.

"Where are you going? Come and sit with me, please," Lucinda pleaded.

"Oh! Okay," Maya said as she sat down with her granddaughter.

"I went to see the horses today. They are beautiful and regale. They are such glorious creatures. I hope that I'm permitted to get close to them?" Lucinda asked.

"Yes, of course, my dear, you're permitted to go close to them. We bought them a week after I took you home. Grandpa needed something to ease his movement henceforth, and me too, whenever necessary," Maya replied.

"I love the both of them," Lucinda replied, grinning.

"Oh, you do?" Maya asked.

"Yes, and I'm planning on naming both of them. I've been thinking of a suitable name, but by tomorrow I should be able to come up with something," Lucinda replied.

"I'm fine with that," Maya replied.

"While I am here, Mom called again, and this time it felt like something was bothering her. She is sad about something," Lucinda replied.

"You mean Annalise, my daughter?" Maya asked, not entirely surprised anymore.

"Yes, my mom. I felt she was sad that I am taking time to find where she is," Lucinda replied.

"How do you know this voice is your mom's voice?" Maya asked.

"If you hear my mom's voice, can you recognize it?" Lucinda asked.

"Sure, I can. She is my daughter," Maya replied.

"Yes, it's true. She is your daughter, and you lived with Annalise for many years. So, you can recognize her voice when she speaks. That's the same way I can recognize her voice because she has been with me for a decade since she gave birth to me." Lucinda replied.

"So, if you find her, will you tell me where she is?" Maya asked.

"If she agrees to it, I will only tell Grandpa since you don't believe me," Lucinda replied.

"I believe you. You haven't lied to us before, so you can't start lying now or cooking up some stories. I believe you, dear." Maya replied.

"Wow! Thanks for believing me." Lucinda replied, smiling.

"You're welcome," Maya said as she hugged Lucinda.

"Now eat your food, my dear," Maya said, smiling.

Maya sat still as she watched Lucinda eat her food. She silently thought of the possibility of Greg being right after all and that Annalise is back. The fact is that only Lucinda can hear her mother's voice. She looked out the window as she continued speaking to herself: I made a wish that you come back.

I don't know how, but come back for your daughter. Guess you heard me. If truly you're back, Annalise, don't go, stay with your daughter, stay as long as you can even if we can't see you. Your presence has changed her a lot and is bringing back the old Lucinda who we know."

∞ ∞ ∞

Chapter 7

Lucinda stood up from the bed

Lucinda stood up from her bed and brought the lantern close to her. Slowly and noiselessly, she opened the door and walked out through the back door. Her grandparents were already sleeping, so Lucinda didn't want to wake them up. She silently tiptoed to the stable and quietly unlocked it, sneaking inside. She walked to where the horses were, figuring they were still awake as she dropped the lantern on the floor.

"It's me, Lucinda," Lucinda said as she ran her hands on the two horses.

"Lucinda! The voice called again as Lucinda looked around.

"I can hear you, Mom. Where are you?" Lucinda said, looking around.

The white horse shifted closer to where Lucinda was as she turned.

"Lucinda, it's me. My soul lives in this horse," The white horse said.

"Mom, you're in this horse? How come? How did you manage? What did you do?" Lucinda asked.

"Wow! My parent's souls live in these horses," Lucinda exclaimed happily.

"I have missed you. Your dad and I have missed you so much," The white horse said.

"I have missed you too and knew you both were going to come back somehow. I was certain when I heard your voice. Even Grandma said my imagination was playing tricks on me, but I knew it wasn't my imagination. Thank you for coming back," Lucinda said as she hugged the white horse and went back to embrace the brown horse.

"Since your soul lives in this white horse, I will call you Anna, and since Dad lives in this brown horse, I will call him Phil," Lucinda said.

"Your grandparents will think you are losing it," Phil said.

"I will tell them. They will believe me," Lucinda said.

"I doubt, Lucinda. They won't believe you," Anna said.

"What your mother said is true, Lucinda. They won't believe you, so don't bother trying to make them believe you. You're the only one who can hear us. They can't and can never hear us," Phil replied.

"Well, whether or not they believe, I don't care. You're my Anna, and you're my Phil," Lucinda said, touching the two horses.

"You should go back to bed now, Lucinda. It's late," Anna said.

"But I want to spend more time with you two," Lucinda replied, rather firmly.

"Your mother is right, Lucinda. Go back to bed. We will see you tomorrow morning. At least you now know that we are here. You can come anytime to see us," Phil chipped in.

"Yes, Lucinda, go back to bed as we also want to sleep now, too," Anna said.

"Alright, goodnight, Mom and Dad," Lucinda replied as she kissed the two horses and carried her lantern with her, walking out of the stable and locking it properly. On getting to the back door, she slowly opened it as she tiptoed inside and drove straight to her bed, lying down and covering herself up.

"Goodnight, Lucinda, we love you," The voices said.

"Goodnight Mother, goodnight Father. I can hear you all even though a distance separates us." Lucinda said as she smiled and closed her eyes, and drifted off to sleep.

"Wake up, Granny," Lucinda said, tapping her grandma to wake up.

Maya opened her eyes slowly to see Lucinda sitting on the bed.

"Good morning," Lucinda said when she saw her granny was now wide awake.

"Good morning. You're up so early. Is there any problem? Did you have a nightmare?" Maya asked.

"Nightmare? No, rather I had the best night ever. About the horses. what are you feeding them with this morning?" Lucinda asked.

"Wait. Did you wake me up so early to ask me about what the horses will eat, or are you hungry?" Maya asked, sitting up.

"I'm not hungry. I'm talking about the horses. What will they eat?" Lucinda asked again.

"Hmmm. So, the horses are now your problem, Lucinda? Since when?" Maya asked.

"Oh yes, Granny. They had nothing to eat yesterday, so what will they eat today? They should have their morning food before ten a.m. at least," Lucinda said.

"Lucinda, is everything alright with you?" Maya asked.

"The horses need to eat. It seems you will not give me the food to give them. Let me talk to Grandpa instead," Lucinda said she stood up to walk around the bed to get to her grandpa's corner of the big bed. Maya was watching her curiously.

She tapped Greg on the shoulder, waking him up.

"Good morning, Grandpa," Lucinda said.

"Good morning dear. Are you up already? You just woke me up. Hope everything is okay?" Greg asked.

"She also woke me up just to ask me for food for the horses," Maya turned toward her husband as Greg looked at Lucinda with questioning eyes.

"Well, Grandma wasn't saying anything, so I have to wake you up too. What will the horses be eating this morning? They are hungry. I'm sure they had nothing to eat yesterday," Lucinda replied as Greg looked at her with his mouth open.

"Are you joking, Lucinda?" Greg asked.

"I'm serious, Grandpa. What will the horses be eating this morning? They will be hungry any moment from now," Lucinda said.

"The horses are animals, Lucy. They are not humans like us," Maya chipped in.

"Speak for yourself, Granny. Who told you they are not humans? Well, I named the white horse Anna, after my mom; and the brown horse I called him Phil," Lucinda replied.

"Please, hope I'm not dreaming," Greg said.

"You're not dreaming, Grandpa. You both are not saying anything. If there isn't any food available, tell me where I can get some food for them," Lucinda pleaded.

"Lucinda, is everything okay?" Greg asked.

"Yes, everything is okay, Grandpa?" Lucinda replied.

"So, why the sudden affinity to the horses?" Greg asked.

"I wanted to ask that too," Maya replied.

"Let me say; they represent two people who matter most to me in this life, and that's my mom and dad. I'm super excited that they are back," Lucinda said, laughing.

"Lucy is there anything you're not telling us," Greg asked.

"Absolutely nothing. I just need food for the horses," Lucinda replied.

"You just want food, right?" Maya asked.

"Yeah, just food, that's all," Lucinda replied.

"Alright, I will get the food for you," Greg replied.

"Okay, so you will bathe them, right?" Lucinda asked.

"Yes, I will," Greg replied.

"Thank you, Grandpa. I need to bathe now," Lucinda said and walked out of the room.

"Something isn't right with my grandchild. Her parent's death is affecting her. Can't you see it? It's turning her into something else. I'm losing my grandchild," Maya replied.

"No, you haven't lost her. We just have to do whatever she wants. With time, she will understand the real thing that has happened to her parents. We have to play along with her until she is of age. If we try ruining this moment for her, she will go back to reclusion, and it's not what I want," Greg replied.

"For how long will this continue?" Maya asked.

"For as long as she takes to come to terms with the truth," Greg said while getting up from the bed.

"Let me get something for the horses to eat and also bathe them before Lucinda comes for my head," Greg said as he stood up and walked out of the room.

Maya followed suit as she walked straight to the kitchen to fix something for breakfast.

Greg himself went straight to the stable, opened it, and cleaned the inside, getting rid of the horse dungs, before taking the two horses outside to bathe them thoroughly.

He then went back to the stable, refilling the water and stocking up hay for them to feed. When he finished, he took the horses back inside the stable before walking back into the house to have his bath and eat breakfast. Lucinda, after taking her bath, had walked into the kitchen to meet her grandmother cooking.

"Granny, can I ask you a question?" Lucinda said. Maya's heart raced for a minute, but she held herself together so that Lucinda would not see the fright in her eyes.

"Sure, you can," Maya replied.

"Can horse talk?" Lucinda asked.

"That's hilarious. Animals don't talk. No, horses can't talk," Maya replied.

"What if one comes out and claims she can hear the animals speak?" Lucinda asked.

"Maybe that will be if the person possesses some kind of magic," Maya replied.

"Does magic exist?" Lucinda asked.

"Magic sure exists, but I haven't seen one happen. So, I will say it's rare," Maya replied.

"Alright," Lucinda said as she went out before Maya stopped her.

"Why are you asking all these? Did anything happen?" Maya asked.

"I just wanted to know if animals can talk and if humans can hear them; that's all," Lucinda replied.

"Hey, Grandpa!" Lucinda said with smiles on her face as Greg walked into the kitchen.

"Have you...?"

"No need to ask Lucinda. I have done everything." Greg replied.

"Oh, okay, that's very nice of you. Thank you, Grandpa," Lucinda replied.

"So, what are you doing in the kitchen?" Greg asked.

"I came to ask Grandma if animals can talk and if humans can hear them," Lucinda replied.

"Animals don't talk, and even if they do, humans won't understand them," Greg said.

"Maybe you shouldn't generalize. Just because you can't hear them, it doesn't mean they don't talk, and it doesn't mean some people can't understand them, either," Lucinda replied.

"Why did you say so?" Greg asked.

"Lucinda, are you now communicating with the animals?" Maya asked as she couldn't hold herself anymore.

"Oh, you don't call them animals. The horses have names, Anna and Phil, and address them with their names. Just because they are not humans like us shouldn't make us treat them like trash," Lucinda replied.

Greg and Maya looked at each other before Greg said: "Are you talking to Anna and Phil?"

"Oh yes, I spoke to them last night. We understand ourselves perfectly well," Lucinda replied.

"That's not possible," Maya said.

"Speak for yourself, Grandma. You don't always believe me, but I'm sure Grandpa believes me. When Mom was still alive, she always said that nothing is impossible in life.

Just because they are impossible for others doesn't mean it will be impossible for you," Lucinda said as she stood up and walked out of the kitchen.

"My grandchild has lost it," Maya said, dropping the spoon she was holding onto the wooden floor.

"I'm so confused," Greg replied.

"You always believe her. Do you believe her this time?" Maya asked.

"It's impossible. Lucinda can't possibly be talking to animals. Oh God, what's wrong with Lucinda?" Greg asked.

"First, she woke me up to feed the horses, and now she can talk to them. And this morning, she looks so radiant and lively, I'm scared that something bad might happen to her," Maya said.

"I don't know what to say, but I'm not worried," Greg replied.

Maya continued with her cooking as Greg left the kitchen to check on Lucinda.

∞∞∞

Chapter 8

Lucinda, where to?

"Lucinda, where to?" Maya asked.

Maya had called Lucinda over to the kitchen to come and pick up her food. She rushed to the back door and was about to open it when Maya stopped her in her tracks, asking her where she was going with the food.

"I'm going to the stable; I want to eat there," Lucinda replied.

"Lucinda, you can eat here," Maya calmly said.

"But I want to eat there. I want to talk to the horses while eating," Lucinda replied.

"Talk to the horses? How can you talk to animals? You can't even understand their language, Lucinda. No one understands animals," Maya replied.

"Well, I understand them. That's why I want to eat there so I will talk to them," Lucinda said and walked out with food in her hands.

Maya went to call Greg, who was sitting in the parlor, doodling.

"I don't know what's wrong with your grandchild. She said, she wants to eat in the stable when I asked why she wants to talk to the horses. Lucinda has lost it. I'm sure of that. It's obvious her parent's death affected her but has it got to the stage of talking to animals?" Maya raged.

"Where is she now?" Greg asked.

"In the stable," Maya replied.

Greg got up and turned towards the front door exit, as Maya followed him in tow. Both of them went straight to the stable. They opened the door quietly, not to make any noise, and found Lucinda feeding the horses with hay cubes. When she finished, she then ate her food. Maya and Greg closed the door as they walked back to the house.

"Maybe we should sell the horses," Maya suggested.

"I see nothing wrong with her feeding the horses or staying in the stable to eat. The horses give her this joy that we can't give her. They serve as companions to her, and look, she is happy. If we sell the horses, she might hurt herself. We might lose her," Greg replied.

"But it's getting to be too much. Every night and day, she is in that stable with the horses, laughing and talking like she understands them, Maya said.

"If these horses were to be the only thing that can make her happy, then we should leave her. Taking those horses away will spell doom. I'm sure you don't want that old Lucinda who became a recluse because of her parents' death. Let her be, okay?" Greg asked and sat down heavily on the oversized couch, his favorite.

"But...."

"Let it be. She is still a child, and this makes her happy," Greg said.

"Alright, if you said so. Let me water the flowers," Maya said and walked out of the parlor.

****

"Mom, isn't there any way you and Dad can come out of these animals?" Lucinda asked.

"We barely have few years left to stay here. Don't worry, Lucinda, we're okay here as far as we get the opportunity of being close to you," Anna replied.

"How do you mean?" Lucinda asked.

"Don't worry, Lucinda, you're still a baby. Don't worry, but with time, you will be able to understand," Phil replied.

"Okay, if you say so," Lucinda replied.

"Thank you so much, Lucinda, for everything. You made your grandparents show so much interest in us by bathing and feeding us every time, all thanks to you," Phil said.

"That's the least I can do, Dad. You and Mom live in the body of these horses, so I have to help. Grandma was even surprised when I told her I was coming to eat here. I can't explain anymore because they don't believe me. They think I'm going nuts," Lucinda replied.

"Lucinda, you don't expect them to believe you because they can't hear us. You're the only one who can hear us," Anna said.

"Okay. Should I get more hay cubes for you both?" Lucinda asked.

"Thank you, Lucinda. You're a daughter who is worth more than gold. Heaven blessed the day I gave birth to you. You have proven to be more than just our daughter, and luckily for us, you're blessed with exceptional wisdom. Thank you so much, Lucinda," Anna said.

"You're welcome," Lucinda replied, smiling.

"Can you take us outside? I need to feel the sun on my skin," Anna pleaded.

"Sure, that's not a problem," Lucinda said as she opened the small door and held onto the two ropes, walking out with the horses.

"Wow! It feels like ages," Anna said, sitting on the grass.

"I'm glad you like it. That reminds me, Dad, Grandpa gave me a silver bottle, and when I opened it, it contained ashes. When I asked, he said it's a gift from you both," Lucinda replied.

"Yeah, he is right. Keep that bottle safe with you. It's parts of us. It belongs to us," Phil replied.

"Your Grandpa is coming, and don't try convincing him because he won't believe you," Anna said.

Greg walked closer to where Lucinda was and said to her: "What if these horses run away?"

"They won't run away. Who leaves their house to go to a stranger's home?" Lucinda replied.

"I don't understand," Greg said.

"This is their home now, so they are fine here. They can't run away when a part of them lives here," Lucinda replied.

"How old are you again?" Greg asked with great surprise.

"I'm still ten but will turn eleven in a few months," Lucinda replied, smiling.

"Please take them inside," Greg pleaded.

"They wanted to feel the sun on their skin. When they are okay, they will inform me so I can take them inside," Lucinda replied.

"They will let you know?" Greg asked.

"Yes, they will let me know. Don't worry, Grandpa. I got this. Nothing is happening to them while I'm here, and trust me, they will not run away," Lucinda replied.

"But...."

"Do you trust me, Grandpa?" Lucinda asked.

"I do, but...."

"No, buts. Just know that nothing is happening to them," Lucinda replied as Greg looked around and walked away slowly.

Greg walked inside and called Maya, and together they went to the window to observe Lucinda.

"What's Lucinda doing with the horses?" Maya asked.

"According to her, she said the horses wanted to feel the sun on their skin, and that was why she brought the horses out," Greg replied.

"But what if they run away? She can't possibly handle two horses. She is just ten," Maya said.

"Same thing I asked her, but she reminded me that nothing of such will ever happen. But then it's awkward that the horses are so calm whenever they are with her," Greg observed.

"Wow! Indeed, nothing is impossible. I'm not talking to her about this attachment with the horses anymore," Maya said.

"Since she finds so much joy and peace in doing all these things, then we shouldn't interfere, but we should watch her closely," Greg said.

"Let me call her so she can have her lunch," Maya said.

"Alright. No problem," Greg said as she watched Maya walk out of the house.

Maya went out towards where Lucinda was with the horses and asked her to come and eat her lunch.

"I'm coming, Granny, just let me take them into the stable," Lucinda replied.

Maya stood still as she watched Lucinda lead the horses inside. She came out a few minutes later, and together she and Maya walked into the house. Lucinda walked straight to the kitchen as she washed her hands, took the plate containing her food, and walked into the parlor.

Lucinda sat on the smaller couch and ate her food silently. When she finished, she walked back into the kitchen and washed the plate before dropping it in its place.

"Where to again?" Maya asked as she saw Lucinda leaving the kitchen.

"Please don't tell me you're going back to the stable. Try to have some rest, Lucinda," Maya said.

"I'm not going to the stable. I'm going to the room to sleep," Lucinda replied.

"Alright, go and sleep, dear," Maya said as she watched Lucinda walk straight into the room.

Lucinda laid down as she closed her eyes. Before she knew it, she drifted off to sleep.

****

"I can't find them. Where could they be?" Lucinda asked, wailing.

"But we left them here," Greg said.

"They are not here. Who made away with the horses?" Lucinda yelled as she fell on the floor and cried herself into a stupor.

"Don't worry. I will get another horse," Maya replied.

"I don't want another horse. I want the two horses back. I need them back. Bring them back to me," Lucinda wailed the more.

Greg searched the entire area, but he couldn't find any of the horses. Lucinda was restless, sad, and melancholy. If only her grandparents knew why she wanted the two horses and that her parents' souls live in the horses.

"We can go out and search for them tomorrow beyond these mountain ranges," Greg said.

"No, let's go now; tomorrow might be too late," Lucinda said.

"But it's dark already. How are we going to find them? We have to wait until morning, and it looks like it's going to rain," Maya said.

"More reason we have to go today. The horses can't be out there in the rain," Lucinda replied.

"Please, Lucinda," Maya and Greg pleaded, hoping she would have a change of mind.

"I said no!" Lucinda shouted and woke up.

"Jeez, so this is all a dream?" Lucinda said, wiping her eyes with the back of her palm.

Maya and Greg had rushed inside Lucinda's room to know what was wrong with her.

"Lucinda, are you okay?" Maya asked.

Lucinda stood up and ran out of the room towards the stable. Maya and Greg followed behind as the trio ran to the stable. Lucinda unlocked it and rushed inside to see the horses still tethered to their places. She was relieved that her dream wasn't a reality. She then took turns in hugging them.

"I thought I had lost you both," Lucinda said, smiling.

"Lucinda, what's the problem?" Greg asked.

"I had a bad dream where someone had stolen the horses, and you and Grandma refused to follow me to search for the horses that night," Lucinda said.

Maya and Greg looked at each other and left Lucinda in the stable.

"I told you that should these horses be taken away from Lucinda; she might die. She dreamt that someone stole the horses, and she is acting like this. What will happen if it happens in reality?" Greg said.

"I hope no one takes them away from us. We have already lost so many animals in the past. The person who is behind the stealing should please pity my granddaughter and leave these horses because as it stands now, those horses are her joy and peace," Maya said as the duo walked inside to continue with what they were doing.

∞∞∞

Chapter 9

This whole place was noisy

"This whole place was so noisy that I can barely hear myself," Lucinda said.

"That's why it is called a market," Maya replied.

The three of them had gone to the nearby village market to get foodstuffs. This was the first time Lucinda had gone to the market. Even while her parents were alive, they preferred leaving her at home than taking her to the market.

They were almost getting home when Lucinda called out to Maya: "Granny," Lucinda said, tapping her grandmother.

"What's it?" Maya asked.

"The door. The door is open!" Lucinda said, almost shouting, pointing at the house.

"Oh no, please let it not be that they have stolen our things again," Greg said as they all hastened their steps. They got into the house and went to the rooms to check their belongings, but Lucinda went straight to the stable to check on the horses. When she got there, she saw the door was open. She hurried inside, and the horses weren't in sight.

"Mom, Dad, I'm here," Lucinda said, advancing closer, hoping the horses will come out of their hiding place. But there was no movement anywhere. And on looking on the ground, she saw that the horses' leash had been cut.

"No!" Lucinda said as she fell on the floor crying.

Greg and Maya heard her voice, and they ran to the stable to check what the problem was. They went there and found out that someone stole the horses.

Maya ran to where Lucinda was and held her tightly.

"Why are they doing this? Why didn't they choose to steal something else? Why would it be the horses?" Lucinda said as tears gushed freely from her eyes.

"Don't worry, we will get another one for you," Greg said, consoling her.

"That's the problem. I do not want another horse. I need Anna and Phil. I need them. They are not just horses; they are a part of me," Lucinda said, crying.

"But there is no way we can find them," Maya replied.

"I want them home. Please, Grandpa, help me," Lucinda replied, holding her Grandpa's hands.

Greg was confused about what to do. He didn't know where to start to search for the horses. Maya tried consoling Lucinda, but all to no avail as she was confident of not accepting any other horse.

"Mom, Dad, please don't do this to me. Daddy, can you hear me? Please, you both shouldn't leave me alone here. You're my joy and happiness and peace. I wouldn't have agreed to follow Grandpa and Grandma to the market.

I would have stayed to protect you both. Wherever you both are, please come back home, and even if you can't come home, tell me where you are, then I will come and take you home myself. I don't want to lose you both the second time.

Tell me where you are, Mom. Dad, talk to me, please. This place will be hell without you both by my side. Please come home," Lucinda said within herself as tears continue to gush freely from her eyes.

She was heartbroken. Her grandparents wouldn't understand why she needed the two horses back, and no matter how hard she explained, they wouldn't understand.

If only they knew that her parent's souls live in those two horses, then they wouldn't bring up the suggestion of replacing them with new ones.

"Lucinda, help us, please," The Voice spoke.

Lucinda looked around and stood up with a start, to the amazement of her grandparents.

"Where are you? Tell me please. Grandpa and I will come to bring you two back home," Lucinda muttered in an inaudible whisper. She made sure Greg and Maya didn't hear her, of course. She wouldn't want them thinking of her to be mad.

"That road that leads to the market. On the left-hand side lies a forest, search deep, and you shall find us. Please, be fast. If you waste any more time, you won't find us here," The Voice replied.

"Grandpa! I know where they are. Please follow me. Let's get the horses before they hurt them," Lucinda said, wiping her tears with the back of her hand.

"That's not possible," Maya replied.

"Please, Grandma, believe me, this time, I beg you. I know where they are. If we waste any more time, they might hurt them.

Please convince Grandpa," Lucinda said as she went to where her grandpa was standing and said, "Please, Grandpa, I'm begging you for this. If you follow me, I would be the happiest person. Please don't say no. You're not doing this for me. You're doing this for your daughter, Annalise, and Phil."

Maya and Greg looked at each other as Greg excused himself and went inside. he came out with his hunting gun.

"Let's go; let's bring them home," Greg replied.

"Thank you so much, Grandpa," Lucinda said as she hugged her Grandpa.

Lucinda walked out as Greg followed suit. They had trekked for a long-distance until they got to the part that led to the market. When Lucinda tried entering the forest, Greg touched her and asked her to wait.

"What's the problem, Grandpa?" Lucinda asked.

"We're entering the forest, and I know you haven't even been here before," Greg replied.

"Trust me, Grandpa. She told me they are in there," Lucinda replied.

"Who is she?" Greg asked.

"Let's go, Grandpa, before they hurt them," Lucinda replied as she trekked into the forest while Greg followed from behind. They had gone so deep, yet there were no traces of the horses.

"Lucinda, let's go home. They are not here, and it's getting late," Greg pleaded.

"They are somewhere close. We can't come this far just to go home empty-handed. We have to go home with the horses," Lucinda replied.

"Please, Lucinda, we can't continue; let's go back," Greg replied.

"Where are you? Talk to me, please. We can't come this far for you to be silent on us. Grandpa wants us to go home, and he is right. Please, Mom, say something, I beg of you," Lucinda said within herself, hoping that her mom replied immediately.

"Keep coming, Lucinda. Please don't go back," The Voice replied.

Lucinda smiled as she turned and held her grandfather's hand and continued leading him deeper into the forest.

"I think I saw them," Lucinda said as she ran closer to where the horses were and hugged them.

"Grandpa, help me untie them." Lucinda pleaded as Greg helped in untying the ropes.

"I'm so glad you both are safe," Lucinda said, touching the white horse.

"Thank you for coming for us," Phil said.

"I don't know what would have happened if you had gone back. Thank you, Lucinda," Anna said.

"You don't need to thank me. I'm simply glad you both are safe," Lucinda replied smiling.

"Who is thanking you," Greg asked, surprised.

"Oh, they are thanking me," Lucinda replied.

"When did you understand the language of the horses to know they are thanking you?" Greg asked.

"I can't explain, but trust me, Grandpa, you won't understand," Lucinda replied.

"Lucinda ," Greg exclaimed.

"Grandpa, let's get going," Lucinda said.

Greg carried Lucinda and placed her on the white horse while he used the brown horse, and they headed home. Greg was amazed at how Lucinda was acting with the horses.

****

Maya walked into her room as she sat on the bed and said: "None of our animals lasts too long with us here. They always steal them from us, and just that, these are the sources of joy for our grandchild's happiness. They have also stolen them from us too. I hope they find the horses. I don't want that old Lucinda back. I don't want her staying in her room crying every day. God, please help us."

Maya bent down as she took out the old box and quietly unlocked it. She took out the Seashell and held it and smiled. Maya was happy the thieves didn't make away with the Seashell. She put it back, locked the box, and placed it back under her bed. Standing up and going into the kitchen, she prepared dinner.

∞∞∞∞

Chapter 10

Greg was still confused

Greg was still confused about how Lucinda knew where the horses were as they galloped back home. Suddenly, he felt Lucinda's hand tapping him as he turned to look at her.

"I have been calling you, but it seems your mind is far away from here," Lucinda said.

"Oh, sorry, my little angel. I was just thinking about something," Greg replied.

"Do you mind sharing with me? I can help." Lucinda said.

"How did you get to know the horses are here, and you were saying something about the horses thanking you?" Greg asked.

"When someone does something nice to you or helps in a time of need, what do you normally say to the person?" Lucinda asked.

"You say the word 'thank you'," Greg replied.

"I helped them, and because of that, they said, 'thank you'," Lucinda replied, smiling.

"That's impossible, Lucinda," Greg said.

63

"Since you can't hear them, doesn't mean I can't hear them. We are two different individuals, Grandpa, and one thing that your daughter, Annalise, taught me is that nothing is impossible," Lucinda replied.

"I had taught Annalise, my daughter, that nothing is impossible in this life, and she had taught the same to you. But in this case, Lucinda, I don't think you can understand the language of animals," Greg said.

"I don't understand the language of animals. I understand these two. They are not animals, Grandpa. They have souls. I know you don't understand," Lucinda replied as she caressed the white horse.

"Tell your Grandpa to hold on tight. We are leaving this forest soon before it gets dark," Phil said.

"Grandpa, can you hold on tight? We are about to experience a new ride," Lucinda said, smiling.

"Hold on tight, baby; hope you're ready?" Anna asked.

"Yes, I'm so ready," Lucinda replied as the horses started galloping swiftly through forest paths, and before they knew it, they were out of the forest. It didn't take up to an hour when they got back home and descended from the horses.

"I didn't know they were this fast," Greg said, panting.

"Oh yes, they are," Lucinda replied as she held the rope and took the horses inside.

"We are home now," Lucinda said as she walked into the stable with the horses.

"I thought we were going to die. Those hooligans were mean to us. They rough-handled us," Anna said.

"Thanks for coming," Phil said.

"Anything for my parents; I'm glad that you both are safe. What could be more than that?" Lucinda replied as she took the hay cubes and fed the horses.

"The dogs, rabbits, and the likes of other animals that they captured, we found out that they steal these animals from people then take them into the forest and kill them for food," Anna said.

"That's so cruel. Why would they do that?" Lucinda asked.

"The question is who and who is telling them about these animals and where they are?" Phil chipped in.

"You're right, Dad, but who could that be?" Lucinda asked.

"Many questions that needed answers. You need to eat and rest, and then I will tell you everything you need to know," Anna said.

"Do you know who they are?" Lucinda asked.

"Of course, I do, and I know why they are doing what they are doing. Lucinda, go and rest. We will talk later, and thanks for the hay cubes," Anna said. As she brought her head closer, Lucinda touched her, placing a peck on her and doing the same to Phil.

"I'm making a promise to you both today. No harm will befall you again. Trust me. I will do everything within my power to make sure you both are safe. I know I just turned eleven a few days ago. I'm small but mighty. You didn't raise just any child. You both raised a fighter never to give up even when the battle gets tough. They will not take you back again; I promise," Lucinda said.

"That's a pretty big promise, Lucinda," Phil said.

"You both made promises to me in the past, and you all kept all. Now it's my turn to do the same for my parents," Lucinda replied.

"Your Dad and I love you so much, and we are forever grateful to have given birth to you," Anna said.

"I love you both more," Lucinda said, smiling.

"Now run along, go eat and rest. We will see tomorrow," Anna said.

"Goodnight," Lucinda said and walked out of the stable. She locked it up properly before going inside the house through the back door.

****

"I'm happy that you could get the horses. At least Lucinda can let us have some peace," Maya said.

"Yeah, but one thing still baffles me. It feels like she communicates with the horses in clear terms," Greg said.

"That's not possible," Maya said.

"The same thing I said to her. She told me nothing is impossible and that some things are better left unsaid," Greg replied.

"How did you know she was talking to the horses?" Maya asked.

"How was she able to know where the horses were kept? She said the horses were thanking her, and she knew where they were when the horses were about to speed off. She had to ask me to brace up for the ride and prompt me when the horses started galloping swiftly through the meandering paths in the forest, getting us home on time," Greg said.

"Hmmm. Really? You witnessed these?" Maya said, keeping quiet, obviously pensive. And after what seemed like an eternity, she added: "Ever since Annalise and Phil died, everything about Lucinda changed since she developed an unusual affinity for those horses, finding so much joy and peace in their company.

I'm suspicious of her, too, whether she is a mere child, but I can't keep asking forever because I don't think I will ever understand," Maya replied.

"I'm simply watching in silence as things play out," Greg said.

"Don't worry. Lucinda is safe, and I know whatever is talking to her is a friendly spirit. So, let it be," Maya replied.

"What you said is true, but I need to be sure that I'm not losing my granddaughter," Greg said.

"And who said you're losing me?" Lucinda asked as she came into the room, leaning on the wall.

"How long have you been there?" Maya asked.

"Long enough to know when Grandpa said he feels I communicate with the horses," Lucinda replied.

"Were you eavesdropping on our conversation?" Maya asked.

"Yea. I was coming in from the stable and was about to go into the room when I heard you both talking in here, and I had to eavesdrop," Lucinda said.

"Lucinda....," Maya called out.

"What you said isn't false, Grandpa. I communicate with you, but you both would never believe me. One thing you should understand is that those horses are part of me, and anything that hurts them hurts me.

There is no need to be suspicious, Grandma. I have explained countless times, but it seems you both would never understand. Anna and Phil are part of this family. They are not just horses. I know with time; you both will understand," Lucinda replied.

"We....," Greg made to speak, but Lucinda mildly interrupted him.

"I know you're trying to take care of me; I understand, but no one is hurting me. Those horses can't hurt me because I'm part of them. I'm not going nuts, either. I swear I'm not losing it.

I know sometimes I speak way past my age, but I guess that's how my destiny was mapped out. I only want to be happy, and those horses are the source of my happiness. I'm just sad that you both think something is wrong with me, but I'm okay. Your grandchild hasn't lost it," Lucinda said.

"She is sad. She just poured out her pains and bitterness to us. Even from the tone in which she spoke to us explains everything," Maya said.

"Maybe we should apologize, but I'm still confused," Greg said.

"Let it go, Greg. Maybe this is how fate has mapped out her life," Maya replied.

"I don't know what else to say. I will have a quick bath., You should be through with the food. Then we can go talk to Lucinda together, Greg said as he stood up and walked out of the kitchen while Maya continued peeling the potatoes.

When Maya finished with her cooking, she dished out Lucinda's portion, and on getting to where Greg sat on the oversized couch, she motioned to him so they could go and talk to Lucinda in the room.

Lucinda was standing close to the window looking outside when her grandparents walked in. She didn't bother to turn as her eyes were fixed on the stars.

"Lucinda, we brought your food, and we also want to apologize to you," Maya said.

"Look up there and see how beautiful the sky is," Lucinda said, still focused on the stars.

"They are beautiful," Greg replied.

"You know my parents always said to me, Lucinda, you're beautiful like the stars, although I haven't heard them say that to me for a while now," Lucinda said.

"You don't need us to constantly remind you how beautiful you're, Lucinda, my dear. I'm so sorry." Greg said.

"It's not a problem, Grandpa, and thanks for the compliment. Maybe you both shouldn't be worried about me that much. I can take care of myself. Rest assured no harm will befall on me," Lucinda said as she turned and sat on her bed.

"Eat up, my dear. The food is getting cold," Maya said as Lucinda picked up her spoon and started eating quietly and slowly.

Greg left even before Lucinda could finish her food, but Maya waited, and immediately Lucinda finished eating. She took the plate and stood up to leave. On getting to the door, she turned back to say: "If at all your parents are back like you said and you can hear them, tell them to watch over you because right now you matter a lot to us," Maya said.

"They heard that; don't worry," Lucinda replied as she watched Maya leave the room.

Lucinda stood up and looked at the sky one more time before closing her window. She drank the cup of water that was there as she lay on the bed and covered herself up to sleep.

"You know you're always beautiful, and you shine so brightly just like the stars, illuminating anywhere your feet touches because the light around you shines so bright and gives light to people." It was Anna's Voice that spoke calmly, followed by a gentle breeze that seeped in through the windows.

"I heard that, Mom," Lucinda said within herself.

"Good night, Lucinda," The Voice said again.

"Goodnight, Dad, and Mom. I hope to get to spend eternity with you both," Lucinda said as she closed her eyes and drifted off to sleep.

∞∞∞

Chapter 11

Lucinda had woken up that morning

Lucinda woke up that morning to have her bath as she hurried to the stable. She was eager to hear what her mom wanted to tell her.

When she got there, she unlocked the door and walked inside. She dropped the hay she was with and watched the horses feed on them.

"How was your night?" Lucinda asked.

"Nice, at least we didn't sleep in that forest," Anna replied.

"Your mom said it all," Phil chipped in.

"So, don't you think it's time to tell me everything?" Lucinda asked.

"They only came for one thing, the ancestral Seashell which has been passed from generation to generation," Anna replied.

"Which Seashell are you talking about?" Lucinda asked.

"This Seashell is magical, and it has been passed from generation to generation. I was the next in line to have that Seashell that I would pass to you, Lucinda, but things changed. Our spirits were already hovering, hoping to meet with the Creator when my mother Maya took out the Seashell and made a wish. With her tears dropping on it, she asked that we return anyhow. She wanted us to come back because of you," Anna explained.

"But how come Grandpa and Grandma can't hear you, and I'm the only one who can hear you? I don't understand," Lucinda asked.

"Because she was specific in her wish. She said she wanted us to come back just because of you, Lucinda. The only living thing that breathes here were these horses. That's why our souls came into them." Anna explained.

"So why did they take you both away? Who is behind it?" Lucinda asked.

"Stephen. He is behind all of this. She had lost count of the animals stolen here, which made her stop buying anymore. Stephen had always quested after the magic Seashell.

He is Mom's cousin. He knows more about the Seashell and what it can do. It broke his heart the day the Seashell was handed over to Mom. He always comes to the house hoping to find it, and after each fruitless search, he makes away with the animals he can find here," Anna replied. "So, you mean Grandma owns a magic Seashell, but she doesn't know about its powers?" Lucinda asked.

"Yes, my dear. She only sees it as an ancestral Seashell passed from generation to generation. The Seashell has the power to grant all wishes except raising the dead," Anna said.

"Now I understand it better," Lucinda said.

"And when I said we barely have time here, I meant we have four years remaining," Phil said.

"You mean you both are leaving on my fifteenth birthdate?" Lucinda asked.

"Yes, dear. Don't think we are going to stay with you forever. You need to know the truth," Phil replied.

Lucinda was quiet for some time before saying: "I guess I will see you both later. Let me have my breakfast first." Saying this, she walked out of the stable with her head bowed down. She went straight to her room and laid on the bed, crying.

Maya walked in and met Lucinda in tears. She dropped the food on the table as Lucinda sat on her bed.

"What's the problem, dear?" Maya asked.

"I'm just sad, Grandma," Lucinda replied.

"Sad? What's the problem? What makes you sad?" Maya asked.

"Don't worry about it. Can I ask you something?" Lucinda said, sitting up as she wiped her tears with the back of her hand.

"Sure. Go on," Maya said.

"Can you tell me more about the Seashell?" Lucinda asked.

"Which Seashell are you talking about?" Maya, shocked, asked to be sure of what she just heard because she had never discussed anything concerning the ancestral Seashell with Lucinda.

"The ancestral Seashell that has been passed from generation to generation," Lucinda replied.

"How did you get to know about that?" Maya asked, still in shock.

"Let me say, a wild guess," Lucinda said, smiling.

"Lucinda, answer my question," Maya asked, keeping a straight face.

"Alright, my mom told me about it. She told me about the Seashell that it was to be passed to her then to me, but since they are gone, I guess I will be the one to take it over," Lucinda said.

"Yeah, your mom is right. and since they are gone, you will have it," Maya replied

"Seashell? What's so special about it?" Lucinda asked.

"Just like you said, it's an ancestral Seashell but unique, and it costs a fortune because of the diamond on the body," Maya replied.

"Aside from that, is there anything about the Seashell that I need to know?" Lucinda asked, hoping that her grandparents might know that the Seashell was magical.

"Nothing else that I know," Maya replied.

"Who is Stephen?" Lucinda asked.

"He is my cousin whom I haven't seen for a long while. But who told you about Stephen because I don't remember telling your mom who Stephen was?" Maya asked.

"Are you aware that he is the one behind all the stealing that has been going on here? Well, he is angry that the Seashell was given to you instead of him. Anytime you both are away, he comes here and ransacks the whole place, hoping to find the Seashell, and when he doesn't, he steals the animals so you both will get hurt. The last time he came, he didn't find the Seashell that was why he took Anna and Phil, asking the hunters to kill them and turn them into meat," Lucinda said.

"I know that my cousin was so angry and left the house after I was given the Seashell, but how did you get to know all that, something that happened over three decades ago?" Maya asked.

Lucinda kept quiet and took her food to eat, but Maya wasn't taking that. She was anxious to know the answer to her question.

"Lucinda, I'm talking to you," Maya reminded Lucinda.

"If I told you, you wouldn't believe me, so there is no need to say anything to you. Trust me; you will not believe me. Aside from that, can you show me the Seashell as I want to see it for the first time?" Lucinda asked.

"You want to see the Seashell?" Maya asked.

"Yes, I want to see how it looks. That's all," Lucinda replied.

"Well, not until you tell me who told you about Stephen," Maya said.

"My mom told me about Stephen. She told me everything that happened, starting from when your grandpa gave you the Seashell and how Stephen has been stealing your animals," Lucinda replied.

"That's not possible because I don't remember telling Annalise anything concerning," Maya said.

"You see; you don't believe me. I told you so that you would believe me. So, I shouldn't answer that question, but I have answered you, anyway," Lucinda said and continued with the food she was eating.

"Why were you crying?" Maya asked.

"The truth?" Lucinda asked.

"What else, Lucinda? I need the truth," Maya asked.

"I just realized I had gotten few years to spend time with people who matter most to me in this world. I can't change it, but I will well use my time," Lucinda replied and continued with her food.

"Lu....," Maya made to say.

"Not another question, Granny. You will never understand," Lucinda said as Maya stood up and walked out of the room.

Lucinda ate her food quietly.

****

"I don't know how she managed to get to know about Stephen," Maya said.

"I'm hundred percent certain you didn't tell Annalise about it, so how come she claims her mother told her about it?" Greg wondered.

"The same question I asked, and she told me no matter how hard she explains I won't understand her or even believe her," Maya replied.

"It still baffles me how she got to know where the horses are, and today, I feel there is more to this," Greg said.

"Granny asked for an explanation, which I gave her, but she didn't believe me one bit. I will not lie to make her believe me. I wasn't joking when I said my mother told me about it. I'm serious," Lucinda said as she walked into the room and sat on the wooden chair.

"Lucinda!" Greg called, but Lucinda ignored him, who came back after a while.

"You both think I'm lying to you both or cooking things up. Don't worry. I know that in time you both will understand all these," Lucinda said as she sat down on the chair.

"So, tell me, why are you here?" Greg asked.

"So that Grandma will show me the ancestral Seashell," Lucinda replied. "Oh, about that, wait a minute," Maya said as she bent down and brought out the old box that was under the bed. One won't even guess there was something under the bed or hidden in that old box. Maya unlocked it and opened it up as she brought out the Seashell.

"Here," Maya said as she handed it over to Lucinda.

"Wow! This is beautiful." Lucinda said as she ran her hands on the body of the Seashell.

"Is this real diamond?" Lucinda asked.

"Yes. Sure," replied.

"Maybe that's why Stephen is after it. He just wants to sell it and use the money for something else," Lucinda replied.

Greg and Maya looked at each other and kept quiet.

Lucinda felt something substantial as soon as she touched the Seashell. The Seashell indeed has its powers. She handed the Seashell over to her grandma, who carefully placed it back in the box and locked it, pushing it under the bed.

"Aside from being beautiful, I felt an unusual inner peace holding it," Lucinda said.

"What do you mean?" Greg asked.

"I said aside from being beautiful, I felt unusual inner peace holding it," Lucinda repeated herself.

"I heard you the first time, Lucinda. I only asked what you mean by that?" Greg said.

"It's inexplicable to me too, Grandpa, but while holding it, it gave me this immense joy and peace," Lucinda said as she stood up and walked out of the parlor.

"If it weren't Annalise that gave birth to this girl, I would have said she is some sort of weird person. She doesn't speak or talk like her age," Greg said.

"You know Annalise acted like that when she was at this age. Remember?" Maya replied and smiled.

****

Lucinda went straight to the stable, unlocked it, and walked inside. She walked towards the horses and hugged each of them.

"It seems someone is happy," Phil observed.

"I can sense it too," Anna added.

Lucinda smiled and sat on the wooden chair there.

"I miss you both," Lucinda said.

"We missed you too," Anna replied.

"I spoke to Grandma, and she showed me the Seashell. I can't explain the feeling I had when I held it in my hands, but it is so beautiful, so ethereal." Lucinda said.

"Did you tell them about the magical powers?" Phil asked.

"Even if I did, they would never believe me," Anna replied.

"I knew they would not believe me, but Mom and Dad, I'm making a promise to you both today, even if you both have few hours to spend with me, I promise to make every day count, and as for Stephen, be rest assured that he will never come back here again. I will see to that," Lucinda said.

"What do you intend to do?" Phil asked.

"You and Mom had always told me that nothing is impossible. Let's watch and see," Lucinda said as she smiled.

She knew she would protect the horses at all cost as her parent's souls live in them. She just couldn't stand to watch anything happened to the horses anymore.

∞ ∞ ∞

Chapter 12

You're becoming too close to them

"You're becoming too close to them, spending time with them more than you do with us. What's the problem, Lucinda? These horses are stealing much your time," Maya complained.

"Granny, I already told you; they are not stealing my time," Lucinda replied.

"You eat with them. You play with them. God knows if it's also possible you will sleep in that stable and eat their food. What's wrong with you, Lucinda?" Maya asked, very much disturbed.

"I will talk to you later, Granny," Lucinda said and was walking away when Maya called her back.

"Your Grandpa and I are going to the village close by to get some food. Do you want to follow us?" Maya asked.

"No!" It was an emphatic response from Lucinda.

"Why? You can't stay here all alone," Maya replied.

"I can take care of myself, and I would like to stay back to protect the horses so they won't be stolen again," Lucinda replied.

"I'm set. Let's get going," Greg said.

"Lucinda isn't going with us," Maya said.

"Why?" Greg asked.

"She said she wants to stay here and protect the horses, just in case the thieves come again," Maya said.

"You're joking, right?" Greg asked.

"You know I'm not joking, of course, Grandpa. I'm serious. Take care of yourself, Granny," Lucinda said as he hugged Maya and Greg before leaving for the stable.

Greg and Maya looked at each other with unanswered questions are written all over their faces. They, however, left the house without Lucinda. When Lucinda was sure they had gone, she walked into the house, locked the door, and went into the room. She bent down and took out the box, carefully unlocking the box and taking out the Seashell, running her fingers over it, and smiling before she started talking.

"You've been said to possess magical powers that can grant wishes and make dreams come true. I only need one thing from you. Stephen will come back, and who knows, he might kill the horses immediately and dump their dead bodies here. I just want you to make him forget everything, everything about us, about this family, so he doesn't come back here again for any reason," Lucinda said as tears trickled down her cheeks, allowing the tears to drop on the Seashell.

On noticing the appearance of the Seashell glittering, Lucinda smiled and said: "Though I don't know what this means, I know somehow you have made my wish come through. Thank you so much." She quickly dropped the Seashell in the box, locked it, put it back to where it was, and walked out of the room. She went to the stable and stepped inside and pecked the horses.

"You seem excited," Anna asked.

"Yeah, because I made sure that Stephen isn't coming back here again," Lucinda replied.

"What do you mean?" Phil asked.

"Yes, what did you do?" Anna added.

"Well, I just made a wish," Lucinda replied.

"Lucinda, what did you do?" Anna asked.

"The Ancestral Seashell; I made a wish with it, and I'm sure the wish had been granted because I saw it glitter. I wished Stephen doesn't come back ever again," Lucinda said.

"Thank you, my angel," Anna said as she raised her foreleg closer for Lucinda to touch, which she did with relish.

"Grandpa and Grandma already left the house. They went to the market in the village close by to get some things," Lucinda said.

"That's okay. Why don't you go and rest, Lucinda?" Anna asked.

"Then who is going to keep you both company?" Lucinda asked.

"Don't worry about us; just go in and rest. We are fine," Phil chipped in.

"Alright," Lucinda said as she pecked the horses before leaving the stable. She got back into the house, locked the door, and walked straight to her room, lying on the bed to see her eyes overpowered by sleep.

****

Maya and Greg had walked into the seer's house as they sat down on the wooden chair and waited for her to come out. They had gone there because of Lucinda, just to make sure everything is okay with her.

The old woman walked out as she sat on the wooden stool before them.

"You came here because of your grandchild, Lucinda. You both think she has been acting strangely," The old woman began saying.

"Yes, we are scared because she spends most of her time with the horses, and she acts like she understands the language of the animals. Aside from that, there is nothing else," Maya said.

"Your grandchild is special. She is a young child filled with wisdom who doesn't act her age. Yes, she understands the language of the horses. Lucinda, your grandchild, spends quality time with the horses because her parents' spirit lives in the horses, and she is the only one who can hear them. Just let her be as she is bonding with her parents, and she barely has enough time because eventually, they will be gone forever," The old woman said.

"But how is that possible?" Greg asked.

"Nothing is impossible. Leave the young child alone. She only yearns for the love of her parents, who departed from this world at the wrong time. Just let her be," The old woman said.

"But, how come we can't see or hear them?" Maya asked.

"Annalise and Phil only came back for their daughter, Lucinda. They want to spend more time with their daughter before they finally leave this earth's surface and its environs. Listen, any day you both try taking those horses away from your home, Lucinda might hurt herself. As it stands now, those horses, the brown, and the white horse, give her immense joy and happiness. She goes out to meet them every morning, afternoon and night. She had formed this bond with them that not even you two can break.

Don't separate her from those horses because you can't. She is not going nuts and hasn't lost it; she is still okay," The old woman said as she stood up and walked inside her closet.

Maya and Greg stood up and walked out of the building as they both trekked back home."If Annalise and Phil's spirit live in the horses, why can't we see them?" Maya asked.

"Annalise and Phil only came back for their daughter and not for us. You heard what the woman said," Greg retorted, angry at his wife's stubbornness.

"We have one option, and that's to leave Lucinda alone with the horses since that's where her joy and happiness lies," Maya said.

"Yeah, it's for the best. Annalise will never hurt her child. She is protecting her," Greg replied.

"I worried because I only wanted the best for my grandchild," Maya said as they journeyed back home.

∞∞∞

Chapter 13

When Greg and Maya had Gotten Home

When Greg and Maya had gotten home, they knocked on the door and waited for Lucinda to open. It took little time before the door flung open.

"Welcome back," Lucinda said, opening the door wide as Maya and Greg walked in.

Maya handed a bag to Lucinda, who walked to the kitchen to set it down. She came out quickly and sat on the smaller couch with hands on her cheeks and staring at her grandparents.

"Is there any problem?" Greg asked.

"No problem. I just missed you both, and thanks for coming back early," Lucinda said.

"Do you want to tell us anything? Greg asked.

"Not now. I just need to have some rest. If I had questions, that would be later," Lucinda said as she stood up, walked out of the parlor, walked straight to the stable, opened the door, and walked in.

"Grandpa and Grandma are back. Do you think I should ask them about it?" Lucinda asked.

"Sure. I want to go home and see how the place looks like. We will be back before they know it," Anna replied.

Anna just wanted to see the house and have a drink from the river before their time on earth was up.

"Alright, let's do it," Lucinda said as she untied the white horse's leash, and together they walked out. Lucinda walked to the balcony and tied the pillar's leash while she stepped inside and met with her Grandparent's discussion.

"Grandpa and Grandma, can I ask you both something? Please don't get mad, and promise me you're going to say yes to my request, no matter how weird it may sound to you," Lucinda asked.

"What's that?" Maya asked.

"Are you saying yes to it?" Lucinda asked.

Maya and Greg looked at each other and nodded, and then Greg looked at Lucinda and said, "Yes."

"I'm taking the white horse to our house," Lucinda said. "Which house are you talking about?" Maya asked.

"Our house, the one my parents and I lived in, the one close to the river. Anna wishes to have a last look at the house and have a drink from the river. Then, before you know it, we will be back home," Lucinda said.

"You can't...."

"Grandpa, please don't say no. The only thing Anna wants is to see the family house one more time," Lucinda said.

"Lucida! Please!" Maya pleaded.

"You already said yes," Lucinda said as she ran out of the house and untied the leash, and immediately mounted the horse to race off together. Maya and Greg ran out of the house, but Lucinda and Anna were long gone.

"Please go after them," Maya pleaded.

"Just let them be, okay? I know they will be back soon," Greg said as he held Maya, and they both walked inside together.

Anna and Lucinda reached the family house as Lucinda stepped down and held the leash. They both strolled down to the river together. Lucinda dropped the leash as she watched Anna go down deep into the river and dipped her head into it. After a few minutes, she came out, and Lucinda grabbed the leash and climbed on top of the horse.

"I have missed everything, and that's why I wanted you to bring me here. I wanted to look at where I lived for decades and brought forth this beautiful angel named Lucinda. I wanted to have a taste of this river that wanted to steal my child from me. I wanted to see and feel it one last time. Thank you, Lucinda, for making my wish come through," Anna said.

"You don't have to thank me, Mother. I will always do anything you want because you brought me forth into this world, and I missed you and the river too. I have always wanted to come here. I'm glad I got to see this place together with you," Lucinda replied, smiling.

"Promise me you will come back here someday. I want you always to remember that this place is your home too," Anna said.

"I will always remember this place, Mom. I haven't forgotten," Lucinda replied.

"Let's go home then," Anna said.

****

"It's getting late already. Don't you think you should go after her?" Maya said, pacing around the sitting room.

"She will be back; I know that," Greg replied.

Just as Greg was still speaking, there was a shuffling of hoofs outside, heralding Lucinda and Anna coming home. Maya heard the noise outside as she ran out to see Lucinda leading the white horseback to the stable. She came out a few minutes later and walked straight to the balcony where Maya and Greg were and hugged them.

"Thank you for coming back," Maya said, smiling.

"Don't worry about me. Mom wouldn't let any harm befall me. She only wanted to look at our home one last time. I'm glad I could fulfill her wish," Lucinda said as she smiled and walked inside.

"Don't say a word, Maya. You heard what she said. Lucinda is fine," Greg said as they both walked inside together, locking the door behind.

∞∞∞

Chapter 14

Lucinda laid on the bed, immersed

Lucinda laid on the bed, immersed in deep thoughts, as she kept tossing around. Her mind wasn't at peace. She knew something was not right, but she couldn't place her hands on what the problem was. It was three months before her fifteenth birthday. Suddenly she stood up and ventured towards the window.

"Your heart is troubled because you feel something unpleasant will happen soon," The Voice said

"How do you know? I mean, how did you get to find out I'm sad?" Lucinda asked.

"I'm your mother. I can sense it, but you don't have to worry. Do you know why? Simple: Worry won't prevent what is about to happen. It has already been decreed, my dear," The Voice said.

"What's about to happen, Mom? I knew something was wrong. I can sense it. I can feel it, and I know whatever is about to happen, it won't bring happiness to me, rather pinches of sadness. I'm not strong, neither am I ready to go through any more pain again. I don't want to lose you and Dad again," Lucinda replied as tears gushed down her cheeks.

"I gave birth to a sturdy daughter, and she is smart as well. She knows how to handle things, even in the face of tribulations. You have made life

85

easy for us for these past few years, but the fact remains we can't be with you forever," The Voice said.

"I know you and Dad won't be with me forever, but I don't want you to go soon, but why do you keep saying you can't be with me forever. What's happening? What's going on? Explain things to me," Lucinda pleaded.

"Lucinda, you worry so much.. I know, whatever happens, you're strong enough to handle it. I love you, Lucinda. Now go to bed," The Voice said.

"Please don't go. I need to talk to you," Lucinda said amidst tears. She closed the window and walked straight to her bed to lay down.

"You think I'm strong, Mother? The truth is, I'm not. I have been able to pull everything off because you and Dad were standing right next to me. I can start no journey without you two, and I don't intend to go on any journey without you two by my side.

I know you and Dad can hear me loud and clear. Whatever it is; whatever you're hiding from me, I know eventually you will tell me because I deserve to know every bit of truth," Lucinda said, wiping off the tears on her cheek.

She turned to the other side of the bed as she closed her eyes and drifted off to sleep.

****

"Do you think we should tell her?" Anna asked.

"Yes, we have to. We can't keep hiding it from her. Yes, she knows we barely have enough time to spend here, but she doesn't know we have only three months left to be in this world with her," Phil replied.

"Do you think she will cope when we are away from her?" Anna asked.

"You worry so much about Lucinda. She is off age now. We should be grateful we were granted these five years to spend with her. We have watched her grow, and I know our daughter is a strong girl. She is growing to be a strong woman. I know she will cope without us when the time comes, but we have to tell her the truth before then. You wouldn't want her to wake up in the morning only to come here for us and tell her we're leaving today. Would you? Think of it, Anna. She deserves to know now. We have ninety days left," Phil replied.

"Alright, I will tell her tomorrow. I just hope she will accept it," Anna said.

She has to accept it, Phil replied.

"I will do that," Anna replied.

****

Maya woke up that morning and turned towards Lucinda, surprised that she was still in her bed by that time, but with her back against them. It was already 9 a.m. It was unusual for Lucinda to be on her bed by that time. Maya got up and walked to Lucinda's bed to see her moping in a fixated direction as if in a trance.

"Lucinda, is there any problem?" Maya asked.

"The truth: I think something bad is about to happen, but I don't know what it is. I can't seem to wrap my head around what the problem is," Lucinda replied.

"Maybe you have been overthinking, and just maybe there isn't any problem. So why are you worrying yourself?" Maya said.

"You don't understand, Granny. I can feel it, and I can sense it," Lucinda replied.

"If you say so, and maybe with time, you will get to figure out what the problem is. Of course, I know you can fix it, but even if you can't, you allow it to be," Maya said and walked out of the room towards the kitchen.

"Why is life so unfair?" Lucinda said amidst tears as she got up from the bed and put on her slippers. Then she walked out of the room to the stable. She opened it, walked inside, and went straight to where the horses were and pecked them.

"You still look worried," Anna observed.

"Your face isn't bright. What could bother you?" Phil asked, feigning ignorance.

"My soul yearns for answers. I feel like something is about to go wrong. Please, Mom and Dad, you both should at least talk to me. What's about to happen?" Lucinda asked.

"My little angel, sit down and listen," Phil said.

Lucinda took the wooden stool as she sat on it and looked at her father, expecting answers.

"I wanted us all to spend time together for a very long time, but that won't be possible because we barely have enough time here," Anna began.

"What do you mean, Mom? I can remember you said that to me a few years back. Why are you repeating the same thing now?" Lucinda asks.

"You're turning fifteen in three months, Lucinda. We are leaving on your 15th birthday," Anna replied.

"Although I remember you were telling this about five years ago, still I don't understand. Are you leaving to go where? Where are you both going? Explain to me, please," Lucinda pleaded.

"Lucinda, we were only given five years grace to stay with you here on earth, and the time elapses on your 15th birthday. When we said we barely have enough time to stay with you, that was what we meant.

We wish to stay longer; we wish to spend eternity with you if that's possible, but right now, we can't because we are leaving to our eternal home," Phil explained.

"That's not true, Dad. You and Mom can't just leave me. It's not nice. Please stay with me," Lucinda pleaded as the tears started gathering.

"There is nothing we can do about it. The decision is beyond us. We wanted you to know so you can get ready," Phil said.

"Nothing? You both can't go. I beg of you," Lucinda pleaded the more.

"This is the reality, Lucinda. Accept it. Be strong for us," Anna said.

"There is something I can do. I think I have an idea," Lucinda said, wiping away her tears, getting up, and was about to leave the stable when Anna called her back.

"Forget about the Seashell. It can't grant that wish you are about to make," Anna replied.

"If it can't grant this specific wish, then why did it grant the first one Grandma made?" Lucinda yelled.

"Stop, Lucinda; you're going to hurt yourself." Anna pleaded.

"This wasn't the plan, Mom, Dad. You promised to stay with me every day. Why are you both leaving now that life is getting more interesting? I'm not that strong, you know.

I have been able to make it through all these years because I had you both. You both are my pillar. How do you expect the building to stand straight when the pillar is about to be destroyed? Tell me, how is that possible? It's not," Lucinda yelled again and walked out of the stable.

"Don't worry; she will be fine," Phil said to Anna.

"I hope she doesn't end up hurting herself," Anna said.

"She won't. Your parents are there," Phil replied.

Lucinda walked into the room and locked the door. She brought out the Seashell, holding it in both hands that Maya had given her when she turned 13.

"There is something you can do. Yes, I know it. You granted the first one, and I believe you can still do something again. Please don't allow my parents to be taken away from me, I beg of you. Life will be meaningless without them. Please, I beg of you, grant my wishes please, just this once," Lucinda said, crying, looking at the Seashell, but no light came out from it. She knew that her wish had not been granted. But Lucinda wouldn't give up.

"Keep my parents for me. I don't want them ever to leave, but even if they are going to leave on my 15th birthdate, let them come back someday, please," Lucinda said, crying. She then dropped the seashell on her bed and walked near the window, looking out into the woods.

"Let the universe hear me. If anyone is out there listening to me, please, I don't want my parents to go forever. Life will be ugly and meaningless without them. I want them to stay every day with me," Lucinda said as tears continued to flow down her eyes.

The revelation from her parents had shattered her world. She was restless, sad, and worried. Why would they leave so soon? Where would they be going to again without her? She wondered. And suddenly she started speaking again, this time solemnly, intensely and gravely.

"If I had ever wanted one thing in life, it would be that my parents could stay with me until the end of time. I have dreams, and every dream of mine includes my parents in the picture. So, how do you think I was going to continue this journey without them? You brought them back somehow, and I know anything is possible. I'm just a young girl whose desire is that of her parent's love.

I want nothing more. You on earth. O ye wind, the sun, and fire; tell me, how do I continue this journey without my parents? I have interceded on their behalf. Please help me. They can't leave on the day of my happy day; I beg of you. You all have to hear me out and grant my wishes," Lucinda said as she walked back to her bed and lay suddenly enveloped in absolute solitude.

∞∞∞

Chapter 15

It was just two days before Lucinda's birthday

It was just two days before Lucinda's birthday. She lay on the bed with tears gushing freely from her eyes. Maya and Greg walked in from the parlor and were surprised to see her in tears.

"What's the problem, this time, Lucinda?" Greg asked.

"Please talk to us. Why are you crying, little angel?" Maya asked as she wiped the tears off Lucinda's face.

"My world is about to end. My whole world is crashing," Lucinda replied.

"What do you mean by your world is about to end? Is there any problem?" Greg asked.

"Yes, tell us, please. We may help you," Maya promised.

"No, you can't. You remember when you walked in here a few months ago, and you said if I can't solve the problem, I should let it be? The problem is that I can't just let it be. How do I continue this journey without them?" Lucinda replied.

"Journey? What do you mean, Lucinda?" Greg asked.

"My soul is bitter. My heart bleeds, and I yearn only for one thing: If only the universe can hear me and reverse this process, then I will be forever indebted to her," Lucinda replied.

"You speak in parables. How do we help if you won't let us know what you're going through?" Greg said.

"Your grandpa is right, Lucinda. You're our only eyes, and anything that bothers you bother us. Please, I beg of you. Talk to us. We will help you," Maya pleaded.

Lucinda wiped her tears as she hugged her grandparents. She stood up and was about to leave, but turned and looked at her grandparents and said: "The truth is you can't help even if I explained everything to you. I love you both, and I know that if it were to be something you both can do, you would do it for me. If only I had the power to go back in time, I would do it. Don't worry about me. This is my cross to carry," Lucinda said as she walked out of the room.

Greg bowed his head, exasperated, but wouldn't give up. He knew, however, that whatever was wrong with Lucinda was deep, and he was going to find out.

Lucinda made it to the stable, unlocked it, walked inside, and sat on the wooden stool.

I wish I can change all these," Lucinda said in tears.

"Stop trying to fight it, Lucinda. Be grateful for having a grace period of five years with us," Anna said.

"I'm not ungrateful, Mom. I'm only fighting for what I love, which are you two. You can't understand. Do you think these past few months have been okay for me?

Do you think those smiles were deep down from my heart? While being here with you, I was only trying to hide my pain and anger, but when I walk into the room, I face the reality that you both are leaving soon. How do you expect me to feel? Happy? Oh no! I can't! I just don't want you both to go.

I swear I'm going to fight it, and I will win it; even if you both leave in two days, I will find a way to summon your souls back to earth. That's a promise," Lucinda said as she wiped the tears off her eyes.

"You can't keep that promise. Do you know why? It's impossible," Phil said.

"I have always lived with the orientation from you both that nothing is impossible in life. Since I accepted it as a way of life when I became conscious of your existence, it may be impossible, but to me, it is not.

I do not know whether those are mere words from you both, but it means a lot to me. I have grown with it, and I believe whatever I want is possible to get. And when I said I was going to summon your souls back to earth, I will do it. Mark my words, Dad," Lucinda said and left.

"Where are you going?" Anna asked.

"I will search for answers. I'm coming back, and I'm sleeping here tonight," Lucinda said and walked away.

"She will never accept this. Hmmm, this girl," Anna muttered.

"Same here. I don't think this girl is going to give up. She is hell-bent on doing what's in her mind," Phil replied.

"I don't want her to get hurt. I wish there is a way we can stop this from happening. I'm in the body of a horse, and I'm fine with it. At least I got to see my daughter grow and see her smiling face again. I seriously don't want to leave. I want to stay and watch my daughter grow up to be a woman," Anna whined.

"We both desired the same thing, but it's time to bow to the call of nature," Phil said

Anna turned her head as she lay on the floor. She would miss her daughter, and her daughter was already missing them, although they were still here.

That evening, Lucinda had her bath and changed to better nightwear to make her comfortable throughout the night in the stable. As she took her lantern to leave the room, Greg walked inside and shut the door.

"Going somewhere?" Greg asked as he sat down.

"Yes, to the stable," Lucinda replied.

"It's late, Lucinda," Greg replied.

"I'm sleeping there. Let me go," Lucinda replied.

"Not yet. Sit down first. I want to talk to you," Greg said as Lucinda sat down quietly on the bed.

"What's troubling your infantile mind, little angel? I know this is something deep. Your grandma is asleep on the couch in the parlor, so don't worry. You can confide in me. Please, I hate to see you in pain," Greg pleaded.

"But you won't understand," Lucinda said.

"I will when you explain. Give me a chance to experience your pain with you. I won't stand it if anything happens to you, child. Please, I'm begging you in the name of your late mother, Annalise," Greg said.

"She isn't late yet. Her body might not be here, but her soul lives," Lucinda replied.

"Please explain to me," Greg replied.

"I will explain to you. I will give you that chance to be part of this. Since she was your daughter, you deserve to know," Lucinda said, trying so hard to fight the tears.

Lucinda took time to explain everything to Greg, starting from when Maya made the wish and how Anna and Phil were about to leave in two days on her 15th birthday.

Greg hugged Lucinda tightly as she cried on her grandpa's shoulders.

"I know how you feel. I wish you explained this to me all these years, as I wanted to be part of this bond. It's so sad I only realized it just a few days before their departure, but weep no more, Lucinda. I know they will come back someday. Nothing is impossible," Greg said.

"You believe me," Lucinda asked, her eyes sparkling.

"I believe every word you said now. Trust me, Lucinda. Your parents will come back someday. Since they somehow cheated death to be with you, then they will come back," Greg reassured.

"Thank you, Grandpa," Lucinda said, smiling.

Greg wiped the tears falling from Lucinda's eyes as he stood up and held the door wide open for Lucinda.

"Go and be with them, dear. They need you," Greg said as Lucinda stood up and walked out into the night towards the stable.

"You came back," Phil observed.

"Yes, I'm back," Lucinda replied.

"It's late; you need to sleep," Anna said.

"I know," Lucinda said as she spread out the nylon mat that she came with on the floor to lie on it.

"What are you doing?" Anna asked.

"When I said I was going to sleep here, I meant every word I said, goodnight Mom, goodnight Dad," Lucinda said and closed her eyes.

****

In the morning, Lucinda woke up and left the stable. She went inside to have her bath, after which she returned immediately.

"It's not even been twenty minutes since you left here," Anna said.

"I know," Lucinda replied as she untied the leashes to lead horses outside.

"Sunshine, finally," Anna said, looking up.

"Thank you, Lucinda," Phil said.

"Let me do it today, even though you both won't be with me tomorrow," Lucinda replied.

Greg walked up to them as he fondly touched the white horse and the brown one.

"I will miss you both. I wish Lucinda had explained things to me all these years. I wasn't part of this journey, but here I am, trying to say goodbye," Greg mournfully said.

"He knows Mom and Dad. I told him everything, and he believes me," Lucinda said.

"Tell him we are saying thank you for taking good care of you, and we will want him to continue when we are gone by tomorrow," Annalise said.

"What did she say?" Greg asked, seeing Anna's mouth opening and closing.

"She was only trying to say thank you for being the best to me," Lucinda said amidst tears.

"Annalise and Phil, I know you both can hear me. I love you both, and I hope you both can stay longer. Well, I'm certain about one thing, I know fate will bring you both back somehow," Greg said.

"Thank you, Grandpa," Lucinda said as she watched her Grandpa walked inside.

After spending some time outside with the horses, Lucinda took them back inside as she provided the hay for them to eat while she went inside to have her breakfast. The day went fast as Lucinda kept wishing the hands of the clock will turn back.

That night, Lucinda slept in the stable despite Maya's pleas, but Greg had to convince Maya to allow her to be.

"I will miss you both. Goodnight," Lucinda said as she closed her eyes and drifted off to sleep.

****

"Wake up! Wake up! Lucinda!" Anna said as she brought her head closer to Lucinda's body. Lucinda slowly opened her eyes as she looked at the horses.

"We are still here. At least we got the chance to wish you a happy birthday," Phil said.

"May your days be filled with love, joy, and happiness, and most of all, peace," Anna said.

"You both are not leaving me, right?" Lucinda asked as she stood up.

"Yes, we are. Goodbye Lucinda. Take care of yourself, and know that we will always love you. We will watch over you," Anna said.

"Farewell, my daughter," Phil replied.

"No! Please don't go, not now!" Lucinda shouted as she opened her eyes and watched the souls leaving the body of the horses.

"Please, this isn't fair! Grandpa!" Lucinda yelled, crying.

Maya and Greg heard the shouting coming from the stable as they ran to see the problem.

Maya and Greg walked inside to see Lucinda on the floor crying. Greg knelt close to Lucinda and held her.

"She is gone, Grandpa. She and Dad. They left after all my pleas," Lucinda said, crying.

"Don't worry, they will be back," Greg said.

"I want them back now. I need them back home. Why would they have to leave on my birthday? Why couldn't they stay longer? Why is life unfair? I'm only fifteen, but I have had my fair share of pain. Why is this happening to me?" Lucinda shouted as she left the stable, ran into the house, and locked the door.

Maya and Greg followed suit. "Please open up, Lucinda. We're here for you," Maya pleaded.

"Just leave me alone. I want to be alone. Go!" Lucinda responded.

They tried all they could, pleading, but Lucinda wouldn't budge.

"Why didn't you grant me that one wish I requested? Tell me why. Are you okay seeing me in so much pain and misery?" Lucinda said in tears as she threw the Seashell on the bed.

****

It had already been months, yet Lucinda couldn't accept that her parents were gone for good. She would go to the stable, hoping the horses will talk to her, and after waiting a while, she would leave. Lucinda was hoping for a miracle. Every morning she would go to the stable and stay a time before leaving.

Two years had gone by since the whole incident happened. Lucinda had woken up that morning, and after taking her bath and putting on her clothes, she went straight to the stable. She took out the white horse, climbed on it, and together they raced down to the village. She wanted to spend her 17th birthday in the house where she was born and raised.

She got there, tied the leash to a pillar, and walked into the house to see that everything was neat, which was unexpected. She held her breath, wondering what could be amiss, then walked cautiously into the other rooms.

Later on, she took a stroll down the river. When she got there, she removed her clothes, dove into the river, and felt peace.

This same river would have taken her life so many years ago, if not for her parents' quick intervention. After spending a few minutes in the river, she swam to the shore, changed her clothes, and went back into the house. On getting there, she untied the leash and climbed on the horse.

She just wanted to go back home and cry since the house had too many memories. But she dried the tears from her eyes and forced a smile.

"Keep that smiling face, little angel," The Voice sounded.

Lucinda was sure of the Voice; it was her mother's voice.

"You're back! Lucinda shouted.

"Yes, your father and I came back together. Happy birthday my love. Even if you can't feel our presence, you can still hear us," The Voice replied.

"I can hear you, and I'm coming back," Lucinda said, smiling, as she turned the horse back towards her parent's house in the direction the Voice came from.

The End.

∞∞∞